THE UNCATCHABLE EARL

A CLEAN REGENCY ROMANCE

ROSE PEARSON

© Copyright 2023 by Rose Pearson - All rights reserved.

In no way is it legal to reproduce, duplicate, or transmit any part of this document by either electronic means or in printed format. Recording of this publication is strictly prohibited and any storage of this document is not allowed unless with written permission from the publisher. All rights reserved.

Respective author owns all copyrights not held by the publisher.

THE UNCATCHABLE EARL

PROLOGUE

"You are to go to London?"

Hearing the faint surprise in her friend's voice, Julianna smiled as serenely as she could.

"Yes, Sarah. I am to go to London."

"But..."

Lady Willingham's voice faded into silence as a frown ran across her forehead.

"I am dulled by three years alone," Julianna explained, choosing to be truthful. "It is not that I am ungrateful for your frequent company – you know how glad I am to see you – but you have two young children and a husband who cares for you a great deal. Your duty is to them, and not to me, even though we are very dear friends."

Lady Willingham frowned.

"I have enough time for all of you."

"Which I greatly appreciate, my dear friend, but I must do more than simply live here in one of my late husband's houses with nothing to do and very few people to see. Besides, it is almost Christmastime, and I should like to be in company for the day itself."

The frown which had settled onto Lady Willingham's features did not relent. Julianna continued to hold her gaze, continuing to smile gently, while a wriggling nervousness ran through her frame. Perhaps her friend had surmised that there was something more to Julianna's decision, and was waiting for Julianna herself to declare it.

But I shall not.

"Very well," Lady Willingham sighed, settling her hands in her lap, and looking to the opposite side of the room in obvious displeasure. "I had hoped that you would join *us* for Christmas, but now it appears that you are quite determined to go to London!"

"I am," Julianna agreed, gently, understanding that her friend's reaction came from a sense of sadness over Julianna's departure... and perhaps a fear that their close connection would never be the same again, depending on what happened in London. "If you wish, you might consider coming to London as well."

A small smile touched the edge of Lady Willingham's lips.

"It would be a fine idea but alas, I do not think that my husband and children would be best pleased if I took myself away to London when there is so much to do for Christmastime. I shall miss you a great deal, however."

"I will miss you as well."

The tea tray arrived, and Julianna poured the tea for herself and her friend, grateful that Lady Willingham had not taken the news with too much distress. It would be different for them both, particularly for Julianna, to spend Christmas in London, but it was for the best, she considered. It had been three years since she had lost her husband. In that time, she had felt her heart slowly being constricted with the grief, pain, and shadow that had been her almost constant companions.

She had not loved the Earl of Carsington, but he had been a good, kind-hearted gentleman and she had valued his company and appreciated his conversation a great deal. To be left alone, a little over one year after their marriage, had been a great shock. Something to do with his heart, the physician had said, and that had been the only explanation she had ever been given. After her proper mourning period and, thereafter, her removal to a smaller property her husband had owned – and which had been left to her – she had attempted to settle into her life as a newly widowed woman, but it had not sat well with her. She had never been the type of lady who had been pleased to sit quietly, or to linger at the back of conversations. Instead, she had reveled in laughter and good company, finding that such things brought a light to her spirit and a happiness to her heart which could not be found in any other circumstances. Yes, she valued Lady Willingham's company and friendship a great deal, but it was not the same.

To London she must go.

"Are you quite certain that it is only company you seek in London?"

With a quiet laugh, Julianna handed her friend her cup of tea.

"My dear Sarah, of *course* it is only fine company – and lots of it! I have been so lacking in such things of late, I find that my heart is quite determined to find it again."

"Which I can understand," Lady Willingham replied, quietly, "but I do wonder if you are thinking of matrimony again?"

Julianna shrugged.

"It would be something to consider, certainly."

"Then you *are* going to find a husband."

"No." Speaking firmly, Julianna settled her gaze firmly on Lady Willingham. "No, I am not looking for a husband, Sarah. It is something I must consider, certainly, for while my late husband left me this property and a little income each year, it will not be enough to sustain me into my latter years, should I be blessed with them. But I do not go to town with the singular hope that I will catch the eye of a particular gentleman and thereafter, be courted and asked to betrothe myself to him. My sole intention is to find a little of the joy which I had in company before my marriage, that is all."

Lady Willingham nodded slowly but there was no suspicious gleam in her eye. Obviously, she now believed what Julianna had said.

"Very well. I think it would be wise if you married again, Julianna. You ought to have a husband to care for you – and who could give you children as well, should you wish it. You are young enough and certainly not on the shelf as yet!"

Julianna laughed, her smile spreading across her face as Lady Willingham smiled back, the tension now gone between them.

"Thank you, Sarah, I do appreciate your words of encouragement."

She smiled again, and then quickly changed the topic of conversation to something a little more banal, keeping the subjects of gentlemen and London as far from Lady Willingham's lips as she could.

The truth was, she had every hope of catching the eye of a gentleman while she was in London. This time, however, she was not about to let herself be caught by a merely *suitable* gentleman. She was no longer a green girl in her first Season, no longer a young lady seeking her first match. This time, she was a widow, with property, a small income, and a title. She had no need to rush into a match, and no need to force herself into a situation where she would marry a gentleman for whom she felt nothing, but who was an appropriate match.

This time, she could take her time, and choose a gentleman for whom her heart felt an affection, and who felt something similar for her in return.

This Christmas in London might bring her many things, but whether it would bring her love was something Julianna could only hope for.

CHAPTER ONE

"And thus, the uncatchable Earl of Wileham returns to London!"

Andrew chuckled, took off his hat, and swept into a low bow that had all the other gentlemen grinning.

"Is that truly what I am known as?" he asked, a little dispassionately. "I would have preferred another title."

Flopping into a chair, he handed his hat to the nearby footman and directed him to bring whisky for them all, just as soon as he could.

"What would you have liked? They also call you 'wily Wileham' you know." Lord Arthington asked, raising an eyebrow in Andrew's direction. "I think being known as uncatchable makes you a gentleman of particular interest!"

Andrew chuckled and lifted his shoulders.

"Perhaps. I would have preferred to be known as 'the dastardly rogue' or something akin to that. I think that makes an excellent impression upon the *ton*."

"You mean that many of them would avoid you altogether, shielding their daughters from your grasp."

Gesturing to Lord Dorchester, Andrew grinned.

"Precisely, old boy, and that is exactly what I want. I do not, at this present moment, enjoy being known as 'the uncatchable gentleman' for it means that there are many in society who are quite determined that *they* will be the one who will be able to break that particular title. Thus, instead of keeping their daughters back from me, they continually push them in my direction. This Season has been most aggravating and, thus, you now find me in London for the winter months in the hope that I will find a little more enjoyment and a little less eagerness from the mothers and daughters who have also returned to London."

"I see."

Lord Dorchester did not look particularly convinced, but Andrew merely shrugged, thinking very little of Lord Dorchester's opinion. An arched eyebrow sent in Lord Arthington's direction made his friend grin and Andrew settled back into his chair with a sigh.

"It has been much too long since I have sat here in White's," he remarked calmly. "Have you been in London for long, Dorchester?"

"Just a sennight." Lord Dorchester sniffed, clearly still a little put out by Andrew's remarks regarding the name which society had offered him. "My mother is present also."

"Oh. I must assume that is not particularly pleasant for you."

Andrew grinned and after a moment, Lord Dorchester offered a wry smile, his icy demeanor cracking.

"She insisted," he sighed, closing his eyes, and passing one hand over them for a few moments. "I planned to come to London to take myself from her company, and yet now she is nothing but determined to linger by my side!"

"There is only one solution to that, you know," Lord Arthington said, quietly. "You must marry."

Much to Andrew's surprise, Lord Dorchester did not immediately rise up and state that he certainly would do nothing of the sort! Instead, he sighed again and shook his head, grimacing as he did so.

"It is the only way that I can see also," he admitted as an uncomfortable prickling ran up Andrew's spine. The three of them – himself, Lord Dorchester, and Lord Arthington – had been friends since their time at Eton as boys and, thus far, none of them had shown the slightest interest in matrimony. Yes, Lord Dorchester had called to take tea with many a young lady, and he had courted a Miss Newforth for a short while, but that had come to an end. Since that time, he had done nothing to further his connection to any young lady. Lord Arthington was much too inclined towards the young ladies of the *ton* and was beginning to garner a reputation for himself as a scoundrel, which meant that very few young ladies would be genuinely interested in his company, and Andrew had simply shown no interest in any young lady whatsoever. Yes, he had danced and conversed with many, but he had not danced twice with anyone, had never asked to take tea with them, walked with them in the park, or even thought about courtship.

Were things now about to change?

"I hardly think you ought to marry simply so you might put your mother into the Dower House," he said, as the footman brought a tray, containing measures of whisky in clear, crystal glasses, towards them. "There must be another solution."

"There is not," Lord Dorchester answered, a little miserably. "I have no real desire to marry, as you know. I will admit that my eye has caught upon one or two particular young ladies this last Season, but I fear that, should I choose one to marry, they will turn out to be just as my mother is... and that is something I could not bear."

Andrew nodded fervently.

"I quite understand. There is a truth in your words – many a young lady hides her true character from the gentlemen she surrounds herself with, so that they do not see her flaws and failures. It is only when marriage comes that they reveal their true nature and thereafter, it is nothing but pain and sorrow."

A scowl darkened his face and, try as he might, he could not keep the flare of anger from licking up through his heart. He had seen it with his own parents, for his mother had been a shrew, and nothing but a drain on his father. It was, to Andrew's mind, the reason for his father's loss of joy, of all happiness until, as the years went on, he finally gave in to the shadows and became nothing but dust. Upon his father's death, Andrew had immediately sent his mother to the Dower House to reside, even though he himself was unwed. It had not been a punishment, but a simple understanding that he could not endure her nagging, ill-tempered ways, which had stolen the life of his father.

"You are thinking of your mother again, are you not?" Lord Arthington took a sip of his brandy. "I will remind you again that not all young ladies are as your mother was."

"But you have no true experience of that, my dear friend," Andrew pointed out, a trifle acerbically. "The ladies that you chase –indeed, the ladies who step into your arms reveal their true selves, certainly. But they are not the sorts of ladies that one might consider courting or even marrying. Is that not so?"

Lord Arthington hesitated before he answered, then acknowledged Andrew's statement with a nod.

"Yes, I suppose that is true."

"Then you can understand, I am sure, why I say such things. The ladies who seek to marry, the young ladies who are presented to us as elegant, genteel, and more than respectable do not show their character in all that it is. We do not see their ill-temper, their desire to nag and pick until they get whatever it is they desire. Nor do we see their disdain for us, for they play their part so well before they wed that we are entirely oblivious to it."

"Some are certainly not as virtuous as they appear," Lord Arthington answered, with a grin. "I can attest to that."

"I do not find the words of either of you to be at all helpful," Lord Dorchester sighed, as Andrew chuckled, his dark mood quickly forgotten. "I am considering marriage because it is the only way that I can remove my mother from my house. I must keep my true intentions a secret for whichever young lady I settle upon cannot know of it."

Andrew spread his hands.

"Should you like us to aid you in your search for a suitable young lady? I am sure that Lord Arthington would be able to tell you of those you ought to avoid, at least!" This was said with a wink in Lord Arthington's direction, but Lord Dorchester only groaned and put his head in his hands.

"I can *certainly* do so," Lord Arthington answered, chuckling. "What do you desire as regards your future bride?"

Lord Dorchester lifted his shoulders and let them fall.

"She must be pretty enough to catch my attention, of course."

"Of course." Andrew lifted his whisky and took a sip. "What else? Do you wish her to be an excellent conversationalist or someone who is a little quieter?"

"A little quieter, I think." Lord Dorchester shifted in his chair, seemingly now a little more satisfied with the conversation. "I am not a gentleman inclined to much noise and rambunctiousness and, whilst I enjoy society, I do not want to overindulge, as it were."

Andrew laughed softly.

"Have no fear, Dorchester, we well understand your desire to stay at home and read a good book, accompanied by a roaring fire and the very best French brandy you can purchase."

"Such has been the bane of our lives ever since we were old enough to make our way into society!" Lord Arthington added, and the three gentlemen laughed together, though Lord Dorchester lacked enthusiasm. Seeing that his friend was serious about his decision to find a wife, Andrew chose to be more serious, and wiped the smile from his face.

"I shall support you in whatever way you desire, old friend," he said honestly. "If you wish to find a wife so that you might remove your mother from your house, then that is precisely what we shall aid you to do. Though I do hope that you will not replace one shrew with another!"

"I shall hope for the same," Lord Dorchester answered, his own smile still a little wearied. "And you are quite certain that *you* will remain entirely unwed as yet, Wileham?"

Andrew nodded fervently, a shiver running down his spine at the thought of standing up in church and making promises to a young lady he would be bound to until death.

"I can give you my promise, Dorchester, that I shall continue as I have always done, giving my attention to no one in particular, refusing to take tea, and only standing up to dance upon brief occasion. I shall continue to be known as 'the uncatchable gentleman' – despite my aversion to the title – and will return to London in the spring Season, just as unattached as I am at present."

Lord Arthington lifted one eyebrow.

"And what if a young lady should catch your eye?" he asked, as Andrew snorted. "There are many pretty faces in London at present and, since there will be Christmas balls and mistletoe boughs, there will be much opportunity for some kisses to be taken and embraces to be offered."

A shrug lifted Andrew's shoulders.

"If I am offered an embrace and if I am permitted to steal a kiss then I shall do so without hesitation," he stated, firmly. "But to do more than that, to let my interest be piqued, my head turned, and my heart yearn for one particular lady is something which I shall *never* do. I have no interest in marriage, Arthington." Throwing back the rest of his whisky, he set the glass back on the table with a bang. "No matter how pretty a young lady may be, no matter how much she attempts to garner my interest, I will be aloof and disinterested. I shall remain unattached and uncatchable for the rest of my days, I am sure."

CHAPTER TWO

The hem of her dress was dirty and damp, but Julianna did not care. To walk back through the streets of London, and to be present amongst society again was a joy that she could not quite express. Her hands clasped lightly in front of her as she turned around slowly, taking in everything from the tall houses reaching up to the sky on either side, the marble lions which stood outside London home which she had inherited from her late husband, and the gentle flakes of snow which had only just started to fall.

"How very happy I am."

Murmuring to herself, Julianna turned and hurried back towards the townhouse, seeing the servants waiting for her. She did not want them to wait outside for too long, and get wet and cold. Hurrying inside, she smiled as the butler and housekeeper came to greet her. She had been given this London townhouse as well as her small house in the country by her late husband's will, and since she had made sure that the staff were retained in each house, the butler and housekeeper were familiar faces, albeit a little older than the last time she had seen them.

"Good afternoon, Lady Carsington. I do hope that your drive was not too unpleasant?"

"I was grateful for the hot bricks, certainly!" Julianna declared, for the carriage had been very cold indeed. "Is there a hot bath prepared?"

"There is, my Lady. We have everything ready for you, as you requested." The housekeeper gestured to the stairs. "Whenever you are ready, my Lady."

"I am ready now," Julianna declared, grateful that being inside the house offered her a little more warmth. "The journey was long, but I am glad to be here now. Are my things in my room already?"

"Yes, my Lady," the butler confirmed. "Your lady's maid has begun unpacking already. There are some invitations which have arrived also, which I have set in the parlor for you."

Julianna smiled warmly, delighted with the news that she already had invitations to various balls and soirees. News of her impending arrival had been sent to one or two friends, and they must have put it around society.

"How wonderful. I will take my bath and, thereafter, look at the letters. Might you have some refreshment sent to the parlor also once my bath is completed?"

The butler nodded, and Julianna went up the staircase, ready to sink into hot water and force the chill from her bones. The aches which came from sitting in a carriage for a long time would fade away, and she would finally be able to relax after what had been days of traveling. She was back in London now, however, and that was bringing her a great deal of joy.

"My dear Lady Carsington!" Warm hands grasped Julianna's, and a face wreathed in smiles faced her. "I did hear a whisper that you were to come back to town – you cannot know how glad I am to see that it is true!"

"It is true," Julianna answered, smiling at Lady Gilford. "It has been a long time since I have been in London, however, and I thought coming at a quieter time might suit me better than coming for the Season!"

"Of course, I quite understand." Lady Gilford finally released Julianna's hands, but then slipped her arm through Julianna's, reverting to the manner of the close acquaintance which they had shared when they were both coming out. "And is this your first outing to society?"

"It is. I was very grateful to Lord and Lady Thurston for inviting me. I did write to Laura – I mean, Lady Thurston – about my arrival, however."

"I do not think that she would mind in the least if you called her Laura, and I will insist that you call me Marianne," Lady Gilford stated with a smile. "We are old friends, and though we have not seen each other for some years, I will always think of you as my very dear friend."

Julianna smiled and let the churn of nervousness in her stomach begin to settle.

"Thank you, Marianne. I do appreciate it very much. I have been so long away from company that I confess to being quite lost with anxiety!"

Lady Gilford squeezed her arm a little more tightly.

"You need not be worried, not when you are amongst friends. Tell me, however, has it been very difficult for you?"

Much to Julianna's surprise, a heat rose behind her eyes, and she fought not to let any tears fall.

"It has been a struggle," she admitted, softly. "To lose one's husband is trying enough, but I lost a good deal more than that. Whilst I was given a smaller property, and the house in London, in my husband's will, the home we had established together was no longer mine. The company of those living in the area surrounding it, the friends and neighbors, was no longer available to me. The new Lord Carsington is most generous, of course, for he made certain that all I was to be given was secured for me without question, but the loneliness and the solitude has been more difficult to bear than I expected."

"I can quite understand that."

Julianna took a breath.

"I was blessed with Lady Willingham and her family, who own the estate near my home. She and I have spent many hours together over these last few years, and I know that she was sorrowful that I would not be present for this Christmas. Her generosity and friendship have been the only things which have kept me from despair, I am sure." A sudden wave of homesickness washed over her, and she forced a smile in the hope that it would encourage the feeling to fade all the more quickly. "But I have come to London to find a little new happiness, a little brightness, and I am certain that I shall discover it, especially with Christmas being so near."

Lady Gilford giggled as though she were a green girl again.

"Do you know that Lord Gilford begged me to come out into the garden this afternoon and, though I protested, saying it was much too cold, he convinced me to do so. The very moment I stepped outside, before I had even taken a single breath of crisp winter air, he threw a mound of snow at me, and it caught me full in the face!" She giggled again, giving Julianna the impression that she did not mind in the least what had happened and was, in fact, rather pleased that Lord Gilford had done such a thing. "We did have a very enjoyable time, once I had brushed the snow from my face," Lady Gilford finished. "Though my hands were very cold indeed!"

"I can imagine," Julianna smiled. "You sound very contented with your husband."

"I love him," Lady Gilford stated, quite simply, "and he loves me, and I find that to be a very contented state of being." Julianna did not reply to this remark, but let the words ring around her mind instead. What Lady Gilford had said was precisely what she herself was hoping for, though she had not admitted it aloud to anyone as yet. "Oh, good gracious."

Lady Gilford's remark made Julianna stiffen, pulling her attention away from her thoughts and returning them to her friend instead.

"What is it?"

"Do you know that gentleman?"

Lady Gilford did not point, but set her gaze to the left and, following that gaze, Julianna took in a tall, broad-shouldered fellow who was, at present, wearing such a wide smile that it shot sparks into his vivid green eyes. His cheeks were a little flushed and as he laughed, his dark hair threw itself back carelessly, bouncing lightly across his forehead.

Heat rose within her like a furnace, and she quickly pulled her gaze away, noticing how her friend frowned.

"No, I do not know him."

"It is Lord Wileham." Lady Gilford clicked her tongue. "He has often been in London, and yet has never once shown any interest in matrimony."

Julianna blinked, then frowned.

"That is not so surprising, is it? There are many gentlemen who do not seek marriage."

"Yes, but they are not all as much of a flirt as Lord Wileham," Lady Gilford remarked, rather more sternly than Julianna had expected. "He comes to London, places himself directly in conversation with the most *eligible* of young ladies, smiles, laughs, teases and even winks at them all! He will stand up to dance, but never dances twice with the same lady! Even though his compliments are many, his murmured whispers of interest and the like spoken into the ears of many a young lady, he has never *once* shown even the slightest true interest in a young lady of the *ton*. Instead, he enjoys teasing and flirting his way through London, revels in the attention given to him, and seems to think that this an entirely appropriate way for a gentleman of the *ton* to behave."

Letting her gaze drift back towards Lord Wileham, Julianna considered him again. Lord Wileham was a very handsome gentleman indeed, she had to admit. The fellow had flashing green eyes and when he smiled, it lit his features with an obvious happiness.

And then, Lord Wileham lifted his head and looked directly at her, and heat shot through Julianna's frame, such was the intensity of his gaze. That smile turned into a grin, as though he was pleased by her scrutiny, and Julianna swallowed hard, aware of the impact his attention towards her was having but, at the same time, refusing to be the one to look away first. She was not some girl in her first Season, blushing and demure, but a widow, one who had been wed before, one who knew what it was to be a wife. A smile from a gentleman was not about to make her weak at the knees!

"Look how he gazes at you." Lady Gilford snorted in

derision. "He thinks that a smile – goodness, a wink! – will make you blush, just as every other young lady has done."

"Thankfully, I am no innocent young lady," Julianna murmured, though the wink that Lord Wileham had sent in her direction was having a most unpleasant and unexpected effect upon her. A bubbling warmth was beginning to settle in her core, and her face felt a little hot. "Ah, there we are now. He has turned his attention to another."

It was with relief that she finally pulled her gaze away from Lord Wileham, and smiled instead at Lady Gilford. She would never admit it to her friend, but she certainly did feel a good deal of interest in Lord Wileham, but that, Julianna identified, came solely from the awareness of how handsome a fellow he was. There was no substance to him, however, not from what Lady Gilford had said and thus, Julianna had every intention of thrusting him from her mind.

"Look, there is Lady Thurston." Gesturing over Julianna's shoulder, Lady Gilford smiled and waved a hand lightly. "Shall we go and speak with her?"

"I should like to, very much." Julianna turned a little and smiled as Lady Thurston began to come towards them. "It has been–"

"Good evening, Lady Gilford." Julianna spun around to see that not only was Lord Wileham standing in front of them, but he was also grinning broadly and, rather than looking at Lady Gilford, was now directing his attention towards her. "I saw you both looking over at me and thought it would be best to come and see what it was you were discussing," he stated, his manner very bold as he let his gaze drift from Julianna to Lady Gilford and back again. "Though we have not yet been introduced, which is most unfortunate."

"Indeed, it is." Julianna threw a glance at Lady Gilford, noting how stiff her frame had become and how her smile was barely held in place. "Lady Gilford?"

Her friend returned her glance and then nodded, looking back to Lord Wileham.

"Of course." The stilted voice she used gave Julianna a hint of how her friend was feeling at present. "My dear friend, might I present the Earl of Wileham." She gestured to the gentleman, who bowed. "Lord Wileham, this is Lady Carsington."

When Julianna rose from her curtsey and let her eyes fall upon the gentleman again, she was a little surprised to see a frown settling upon his face, though it quickly faded the moment that her eyes met his again. What was it about her which made him frown so?

"Lady Carsington," Lord Wileham murmured, extending a hand to her which Julianna gave, only for him to bow over it for a second time. "Very good to meet you. Is your husband here with you? I do not think that I am acquainted with him either."

Julianna hesitated, then chose to speak plainly.

"My husband passed away some three years ago, Lord Wileham." Stating this quickly, she saw Lord Wileham close his eyes in clear embarrassment. "This is the first time that I have been in London since his passing."

"I am very sorry for your loss," he said, a flicker of red dancing about his cheeks. "Forgive me, I did not know."

"I would not have expected you to." Was that why he had frowned when Lady Gilford had introduced them? Had he thought – or hoped – for her to be an unattached young lady? "Are you to spend Christmas here in London, Lord Wileham?"

He cleared his throat, now appearing a little stiff in his manner, which Julianna put down to his embarrassment.

"Yes, I think I shall be," he stated, his hands clasping behind his back. "And you?"

"My intention is to stay in London for as long as I still wish to be here," she replied, having given herself no time by which she ought to return home.

Lord Wileham smiled suddenly, a glint coming into his eye, and that curl of heat that she had felt at their first glance returned to her stomach.

"Then I think that we shall see a good deal of each other, Lady Carsington." He inclined his head. "I do look forward to our next meeting. Good evening."

"Good evening," Julianna murmured, watching as Lord Wileham walked away, wondering at his sudden change of temperament.

"Do you see what I mean?" With a toss of her head, Lady Gilford tutted loudly. "He is quite serious one moment and then a complete flirt the next! He wants you to admire him, to seek him out, and when he does not return your interest, pine after him."

Julianna took a deep breath and nodded, exhaling slowly.

"Then he is not the sort of gentleman whom I wish to be acquainted with," she stated firmly. "I do not think that we shall often be in company with Lord Wileham, no matter how much he desires it."

CHAPTER THREE

*I*t was all terribly disconcerting.

Mulling it over his glass of brandy, Andrew let his gaze flit to the amber which swirled from one place to the next and tried not to recall his embarrassment. He had been smiling to himself when he had caught a young lady gazing at him, while her friend spoke earnestly in her ear. While his promise remained true – for he still had no intention of allowing any young lady to attract his affections – he enjoyed catching the interest of the young ladies of the *ton*. It brought him a sense of satisfaction, added to his pride, and took away from the loneliness which, had he the strength to admit it, lingered deep within his soul.

But he had made a mistake when it came to Lady Carsington. First of all, she was not a young, unattached lady as he had at first thought. When she had been introduced to him by Lady Gilford, with whom he was already acquainted, he had been surprised to hear her title. Thereafter, upon asking about her husband, he had embarrassed himself all the more. Over and over, he had reminded himself that he did not need to feel such embarrassment, as it was not something which he could have known beforehand but, all the same, the shame of it lingered with him still. He had tried to brush it off quickly, had tried to regain his former easiness of manner, and light conversation, but it had been difficult.

This was, no doubt, the reason that Lady Carsington lingered in his mind some two days after their first meeting. He had not seen her since, and now found himself desiring to do so, eager to recover himself as best he could.

She was very beautiful.

That was no trouble to admit to himself, for Andrew was a gentleman continually surrounded by beauty. Lady Carsington carried herself with a grace and elegance which many a young lady would seek to replicate, but her blue eyes had held a sharpness which had almost compelled him to gaze back at her. The delicate way that wisps of her light brown hair had danced at her neck had drawn his attention there, also, and he had permitted himself to take her in. Yes, Lady Carsington was more than a little beautiful but what was that to him? He could not permit himself to think anything more of it. After all, his intention was to continue as he had always done, treating Lady Carsington as he would any other young lady, simply for his own enjoyment.

"You look a little dull, Wileham!"

Andrew lifted his head as Lord Arthington stepped in.

"I told your butler that I needed no introduction, and made my way to your parlor without his company. I hope you do not mind."

"Not in the least." Andrew waved his friend's attention toward the brandy. "Help yourself, if you wish."

"Thank you." Pouring a small measure, Lord Arthington took a seat opposite Andrew. "Whatever is the matter? I thought you would have been beaming with delight at the prospect of going to another soiree. Town is busy with many families here – more than I have seen in London at Christmas for some time – and I am sure that you will be able to garner the attention of many a young lady, simply so that you might break their hearts when you show them no true interest whatsoever."

He laughed but Andrew merely grunted, making his friend frown.

"And something more troubles you?" Putting out his hands, he spread them wide in question. "What?"

Andrew heaved a sigh and then shook his head.

"It is ridiculous, of course. I embarrassed myself significantly in front of a lady – one Lady Carsington – and now I feel both frustrated and irritated with my own reaction to that. I feel as though I have lost the confidence which I cling to so dearly, and now must regain myself in front of her, somehow."

"Then do so." Lord Arthington shrugged. "It does not matter if you embarrassed yourself, for every gentleman has done such a thing at some point in his life!" His eyes narrowed. "Did you say Lady Carsington?"

"Yes."

"Then she is a married woman?"

Andrew shook his head.

"Widowed."

"Ah." Lord Arthington grinned, his eyes sparkling with good humor. "Then there is nothing to prevent you from treating her with the same... interest as you do others. Unless she is only just free from her mourning period?"

"He has been gone some three years."

Lord Arthington slapped his thigh.

"Well, then, there is nothing to prevent you from doing such a thing, is there? You will find your embarrassment forgotten and your confidence regained very soon, I am sure. Come now, no more brooding over this Lady Carsington." Getting to his feet, he threw back his brandy and jerked his head towards the door. "Let us go. The soiree is waiting!"

～

"Now, show me where this Lady Carsington is."

Andrew grimaced, running one hand over his chin.

"I do not know if she is present."

"I would be surprised if she is not. Almost everyone in high society has been invited to Lord and Lady Jefferson's soiree, save for the few that they consider to be scoundrels and rakes."

"Which makes me wonder at *your* invitation."

Lord Arthington let out a bark of laughter, just as Lord Dorchester came to greet them.

"Good evening." He glanced from Andrew to Lord Arthington. "What is it that has made you so merry?"

"Wileham is looking for Lady Carsington," Lord Arthington replied, before Andrew could prevent him. "He embarrassed himself in front of her and now feels himself a little lacking. Given that she has been widowed for some years, I have told him that he can simply behave with her as he has done with every other young lady of his acquaintance and that, surely, will return his confidence to him."

Lord Dorchester rolled his eyes.

"Or you could simply find someone else to toy with and leave Lady Carsington be," he remarked. "There are many young ladies here who would be glad of your flirtations, I am sure. Lady Carsington does not need to be one of them."

"That is true." All the same, even though he agreed with

the premise, Andrew refused to permit the thought to linger. There was something about Lady Carsington which frustrated him, called out to him, and captured him and, until he was able to speak with her again, was able to behave with her as he usually did, then he was convinced that this niggle, this continuous scratch, would not go away. "And how are you faring, Lord Dorchester? Is there a young lady whom you are considering?"

Lord Dorchester lifted his chin.

"Yes, there is, in fact."

Andrew's eyes flared, his breath catching with surprise.

"That was a little hasty, was it not?"

"It has been a sennight since we spoke of it. You did not think that I have had my eyes closed these last few months, did you? I was in London for the Season and, whilst I may not have behaved as you did, it does not mean that I was unaware of the young ladies present."

"So you have always been interested in one particular young lady?" Lord Arthington asked, as Lord Dorchester sniffed and looked away.

"I do not know if I would say that. I have been *aware* of her, that is all I shall state. I should be appreciative, however, if you would stay away from the young lady in question, Wileham. I do not want you to attempt to bring *her* under your spell!"

Andrew shrugged.

"Very well. What is her name?"

For a moment, he wondered if Lord Dorchester was not going to answer, only for his friend to draw himself up to stand as tall as he could, lift his chin and finally give the answer.

"She is Miss Sophia Hallstrom."

Having no recognition of the name, Andrew nodded.

"Very well. If I am to be introduced to this young lady at any juncture, I will remember not to wink at her, not to overly compliment her, and not to whisper things into her ear when we dance." A smile spread across his face as Lord Dorchester scowled, and he wondered silently to himself if his friend felt more for this Miss Hallstrom than he was willing to admit. "I shall leave all that for you to do."

Lord Dorchester closed his eyes and sighed.

"Very well. I thank you for that, I suppose."

"Very good." With a broad smile, Andrew turned back to Lord Arthington. "Now, shall we go in search of – ah!" His eyes alighted on the lady in question, the one he had been looking for since their arrival. Lady Carsington was walking arm in arm with Lady Thurston, and they were talking rapidly. Andrew found his lips quirking when Lady Carsington laughed, though this quickly turned to a grin when he caught the sharp eyes of Lord Arthington settling on him. "We have found her," he stated, gesturing towards Lady Carsington though, thankfully, she had not noticed him as yet. "*That* creature, the one walking with Lady Thurston, is Lady Carsington."

Lord Arthington turned and then stood shoulder to shoulder with Andrew.

"I see. She is very beautiful, I must say."

"I would agree." Andrew set his shoulders straight and winked at his friend. "And now I go to speak with her, and to treat her as I do any other young lady, in the hope that doing so will rid me of this little, frustrating, constant niggle as I remember my embarrassment."

"I wish you luck," Lord Arthington replied, though Lord Dorchester snorted in obvious disdain. "Go forth, speak with the lady and conquer this!"

With a smile on his face, Andrew walked directly across

the room, his gaze fixed on Lady Carsington. When she finally caught his eye, her smile quickly faded and, to his surprise, she sighed and threw a glance to her friend – a glance which spoke of frustration at being so interrupted.

"Lady Carsington, Lady Thurston." He bowed, and smiled as warmly as he could when he rose. "How good to see you both this evening."

"Lord Wileham." Lady Thurston murmured, no smile on her face. "Good evening."

"Good evening, Lord Wileham," Lady Carsington said, speaking a little more quickly than her friend. "You must forgive us – we are just now on our way to greet Lady Gilford, who has only just arrived and is now looking for our company! We shall have to speak again very soon. For the moment, however, please excuse us."

Without another word, without so much as another glance, Lady Carsington took Lady Thurston's arm again, and the two ladies stepped away from him, leaving Andrew utterly dumbfounded. No one had ever treated him with such disregard before! He had always merited at least a smile and a few minutes of conversation, but Lady Carsington had made it quite clear that she had absolutely no desire or interest in standing to talk with him. Shock ricocheted through him, and he turned, walking back towards his two friends without really seeing them.

"It seems she had no desire to talk with you, did she?"

Andrew looked up at Lord Dorchester. Was that a hint of mirth in his voice? Was he somehow pleased that Andrew had suffered this embarrassment?

"I interrupted her at the wrong moment," he told his friend, stiffly. "That is all."

"Indeed." Lord Dorchester agreed, but the smile on his face, which he had been attempting to hide thus far, now quickly spread across his expression. "What a pity that you will not be able to rid yourself of this... niggle, as you called it?" He sighed as though in sympathy though his eyes twinkled still. "It seems as though you will have to endure for a little longer."

"Yes," Andrew agreed, as stoically as he could, refusing to shrink in front of Lord Dorchester. Yes, Lady Carsington had thrown him back, had pushed him away from her, but he was not about to give up. He *would* speak with her again, would let himself smile and tease her, until he managed to have her respond as the other young ladies did. Then, he would be free of this frustration surrounding her. "It seems as though I shall."

CHAPTER FOUR

"Would you like to dance?"

Julianna hesitated, glancing at Lady Thurston who merely offered a small shrug.

"You are very kind to ask me, Lord Pleasanton." Her eyes went to the kissing bough which had been placed near the fireplace, but was also close enough for gentlemen and ladies who were dancing to stop underneath. "I should like to, yes, but with the promise that you will not expect a kiss from me."

Lord Pleasanton smiled and nodded.

"I quite understand. There is no expectation of the sort, Lady Carsington."

When he offered his arm, Julianna took it carefully and allowed him to lead her out to the floor. This was the first time she had danced in society for many years and the awareness unnerved her a little.

The music began and Julianna curtsied as Lord Pleasanton bowed before stepping forward so that they might turn one another before stepping back into place. Her feet took to the steps easily enough, her memory of them coming back with great swiftness and, to her relief, she was able to dance without difficulty.

"Ah, and now you smile." Lord Pleasanton chuckled as she looked up at him, only to flush as he grinned at her. "Has it been some time since you stepped out to dance?"

"Years, Lord Pleasanton," she admitted, freely. "Since my husband passed away, I have lived in solitude and, save for some very dear friends, have lacked company. There has not been much requirement for dancing!"

"Then you must make sure to dance at every opportunity," he told her with a smile, as their steps took them away from each other. Julianna's smile lingered, only for it to crack as she was faced with none other than Lord Wileham. The dance had them dancing with another partner for a few short moments and even though she did as was expected, even though she let him turn her about the floor, she did not say a single word to him.

Inwardly, however, her heart was pounding, her mouth going dry, and she dared not look at him. Lord Wileham was the sort of gentleman she ought to stay away from, whom she ought to ignore and yet there was something about him, about his manner that, while she found it deeply frustrating, she was shocked to discover that she also desired that attention. It was most startling.

"Good evening, Lady Carsington. I did not think you would be dancing."

These few words had her eyes turning back to him, only to pull away again.

"There is no reason for me not to dance, Lord Wileham," she murmured, as her steps pulled her away from him again. With relief, she danced again with Lord Pleasanton, and they exchanged a few words about the Christmas Season in general, and how cold the weather was, only for her to be forced back in Lord Wileham' direction again.

"I did not mean to suggest that you could *not* dance," Lord Wileham stated, clearly continuing with their previous conversation. "Only that I did not think you would."

"Because I am a widow?"

The harsh tone of her voice did not escape her and, a little embarrassed, she dropped her gaze to the floor, wishing that she had not been forced to dance with him. She found him confusing, overly bold in his questions, and while handsome, not kind in character. Why was it that she felt drawn to him? It was very strange indeed.

"You are quite correct." Lord Wileham looked at her, as his steps took him away from her again. "I ought not to have thought that a widowed lady could not dance."

"No, you should not have," she answered, before turning to dance with Lord Pleasanton again. Much to her relief, her steps did not take her back in Lord Wileham's direction again and thus, she was able to dance the rest of the set without concern or worry that he would once again be in her company.

"Tell me, Lady Carsington," Lord Pleasanton asked, as the dance came to a close, "while you are averse to a kissing bough, might I ask if you have any aversion to *other* things related to this time of year?"

A little confused as to what he meant, Julianna looked up at him, her hand going to rest on his arm as they walked together back to the side of the room.

"Averse to what things in particular, Lord Pleasanton?"

"To walks in the park?" he asked, his smile growing when she laughed. "To taking tea with, perhaps, a few extra delicacies set out? To sitting by a roaring fire and discussing whether or not the Yule log will be large enough to bring us through into the New Year?"

Her eyes twinkled as she saw the light in his eyes. Lord Pleasanton was a very amiable gentleman, she considered, though she did not know him particularly well, as yet.

"I do not think that I would avoid such things, Lord Pleasanton."

"Even if the weather is very cold?" he asked, glancing at the windows, though the sky outside was dark. "I confess, I enjoy walking through the park when there has been snow – though we are getting a great deal of it this year!"

She smiled at him.

"I enjoy that a great deal also."

"Then would you consider my request if I were to ask you to walk with me through Hyde Park tomorrow afternoon?"

Julianna thought for a few moments, thinking to herself that Lord Pleasanton seemed to be a considerate fellow and that, whilst she had no idea of his true character as yet, he was pleasant enough to make her consider deepening her acquaintance with him.

"I think I should be glad to, yes."

"Excellent!" Lord Pleasanton boomed suddenly, making her jump. "I shall call for you tomorrow in the carriage, which will then take us both to the park where we can enjoy a short walk – should the weather hold for us!"

Julianna let herself smile, aware of the slight flicker of nervousness which warmed her heart.

"If it is a terrible snowstorm, then mayhap we shall have to sit by a roaring fire and discuss the Yule log," she said, making him laugh. "Thank you, Lord Pleasanton. I look forward to our time together tomorrow."

"As do I."

With a bow, he led her back to Lady Thurston, and then turned to take his leave and, perhaps, to dance with another young lady.

"Lord Pleasanton was delighted in your company," Lady Thurston murmured, casting Julianna a searching look. "Did you think him a good dancer?"

"Yes, I think so." Choosing not to hide what he had asked her, Julianna told her friend the entirety of the conversation that she had shared with Lord Pleasanton. "And we are now to walk in Hyde Park tomorrow. I only hope that there is not a great snowfall to deter us away from the idea."

Lady Thurston turned so that she could look at Julianna a little more directly.

"You are hoping for courtship, then?"

Julianna shook her head.

"I am not averse to the idea," she said, smiling to herself as she used the same term as Lord Pleasanton had himself used. "But I will not marry a gentleman simply because he and I rub along fairly well together. There must be more to our connection, more than a simple consideration."

"You want affection, then?"

Julianna nodded.

"I want to find a gentleman who will be open to the possibility, at the very least."

"Very well." Lady Thurston did not argue or question her further, much to Julianna's surprise. Her friend had always pushed away the idea of love and had married a gentleman chosen for her by her late father. Julianna had presumed, then, that Lady Thurston would be pushing her as far away from the idea as she possibly could - but instead, she was simply accepting it. "Then let us hope that Lord

Pleasanton is as good a gentleman as you might hope him to be!"

Julianna smiled.

"Indeed."

"It will be odd for you to walk through the park without a chaperone," Lady Thurston remarked, as Julianna stopped in her conversation, her eyes flaring. "You have no need for one now."

"I – I had not thought of that." Rubbing one hand over her eyes, she shook her head. "Goodness. How strange that will be!"

"I hear you are to walk in the park with Lord Pleasanton."

She turned her head, and a spark rushed up her spine as Lord Wileham' flashing eyes looked back at her.

"Good evening, Lord Wileham."

"Perhaps you would be willing to take a carriage ride with me, then?"

"A carriage ride?"

The request was an extraordinary one, for had Lady Gilford not told her that Lord Wileham was not a gentleman inclined towards such things? That he never sought out a young lady's company in such a way?

"Yes." Lord Wileham lifted his head, a flash in his eyes. "I believe that this is what gentlemen do when they would appreciate a little more time in a lady's company."

This was most extraordinary, Julianna considered. Why would Lord Wileham ask such a thing of her when he had never made a request to any other young lady before her? Recalling what Lady Gilford had said as regarded the gentleman, it did not take much for Julianna to lift her chin and shake her head.

"I do not think that I should be amenable to that, Lord

Wileham," she answered, seeing how his jaw tightened, the easy smile falling from his face. "Though it is most kind of you to offer."

"Might I ask why you will not join me?"

She offered him a simple explanation though it bore no similarity to the truth.

"Simply because I think a carriage ride will be much too cold this time of year and I am so inclined towards chilblains."

Lord Wileham cleared his throat and inclined his head.

"Very well, Lady Carsington. A dance, then. I have only just now stepped away from a Miss Hallstrom and find myself quite inclined towards dancing another set with a new partner."

Having believed herself free of him, Julianna blinked in surprise.

"A dance?"

Letting out a huff of breath – a clear indication that he was somewhat frustrated by her repetition of his words – Lord Wileham nodded.

"Yes, a dance. You have danced with Lord Pleasanton, so I am certain that you have no reason to refuse me."

Julianna fought to find one, to challenge him with her response, but none came. She could offer him nothing, could not find a single answer to give him, other than a positive one.

And thus, Julianna found herself stepping out with Lord Wileham, the one gentleman she did *not* want to dance with. Eyeing the kissing bough carefully, she prayed inwardly that Lord Wileham would not bring her close to it, and determined that, should he do so, she would have no qualms in refusing him a kiss for, to her mind, he certainly did not merit it.

CHAPTER FIVE

"There you are, Lord Wileham!"

Andrew grinned and stretched out his legs, so that they rested on the stool in front of him, his feet pointing to the roaring fire in the hearth.

"Good evening, Lord Whitaker, Lord Rushford. You have been looking for me?"

"Indeed we have!"

Lord Rushford spoke energetically, as Andrew offered a glance to Lord Arthington, who merely shrugged his shoulders. The two gentlemen had been enjoying a quiet drink at White's after what had been an evening of great enjoyment, where Andrew had danced with many a young lady, teased them unconscionably and garnered a great many smiles and longing looks, which had made him very contented indeed. To now be interrupted by two acquaintances in such a loud manner was not what either of them expected.

"You do not know why?" asked Lord Whitaker, taking a seat opposite Andrew without having been invited. "Why, it is only that Lady Henrietta, daughter to the wealthy Marquess of Barrington, has declared herself quite in love with you and is determined, apparently, to make you fall in love with her."

Andrew blinked.

"I see." Trying to bring her face to mind, he shrugged inwardly when he could not. "I do wish the lady success."

"You do not think she will succeed?"

Andrew snorted in answer to Lord Whitaker's question.

"I certainly have no hope of her succeeding. As you are aware, no doubt, I have no intention of allowing anyone into my heart and thus, despite Lady Henrietta's determination, I do not think she shall succeed."

"You do not even know who she is, do you?" Lord Rushford's voice was suddenly accusatory, one finger pointed in Andrew's direction. "You would not recognize her, even if she were standing directly in front of you!"

With a sniff, Andrew lifted his shoulders and then let them fall.

"I am certain I would. I simply cannot recall her at this present moment."

"Which I do not believe," Lord Rushford answered, his words whipping across the room, his eyes a little narrowed. "You do know that Lady Henrietta is a relation of mine, do you not?"

This gave Andrew pause.

"I did not know that there was a connection, no."

"Then you *do* know who she is?"

A little flustered, Andrew shifted in his chair, not wanting to upset Lord Rushford further. The gentleman was clearly in his cups, having imbibed a little too much, and was now a good deal more reactionary than he might otherwise have been.

"I am sure that I would recognize her face, should I see her again."

"Prove it."

Blinking in surprise, Andrew then let a frown settle over his forehead.

"What can you mean?"

"A bet."

Lord Rushford's eyes narrowed, just as Lord Whitaker chuckled and reached out one hand to Lord Rushford.

"Whatever are you talking about? When we made our way to White's, you were laughing about your cousin's regard for Lord Wileham, and now you are angry because he does not recognize her, simply from you speaking her name? Come now, do not be so very ridiculous. There is no need for this!"

Andrew was about to say how much he agreed, only for a second voice to interrupt them.

"But I think a bet is a marvelous idea."

He frowned, looking past Lord Rushford and into Lord Dorchester's face. When had he arrived?

"Dorchester, there is no need for a bet."

"It is not about need, but rather about good humor between friends," Lord Dorchester replied, coming a little closer. "You say that you know Lady Henrietta, that you would recognize her, and Lord Rushford is not certain that is the truth. So a bet is an excellent suggestion, for it will prove one of you correct." A shadow flickered in his eyes. "What say you?"

Andrew knew what he ought to say, what would be wise, but instead, he found himself lifting his chin and nodding.

"Very well."

Lord Dorchester grinned, the shadow gone from his eyes.

"Now we shall see if you really *do* know this lady, Wileham! And perhaps, for once, your confidence and assurance will not be as prominent as usual!"

A knot tied itself in Andrew's throat and he frowned at Lord Dorchester. Ever since Lord Dorchester had announced his intention to find a wife, there had been a change in his attitude towards Andrew. Andrew himself could not quite place it, nor understand it fully, but all the same, he did not appreciate it. *It does not matter,* he told himself as the other gentlemen began to discuss the terms of this bet, and how they might go about proving it. *I will be able to find out who Lady Henrietta is for certain before I have to prove anything.* He could ask his butler for a description, perhaps even call to take tea with her before anyone had any idea that he had done so.

"She is at the ball still, I am sure!"

Andrew's heart slammed hard against his ribs, shock ricocheting through him as he looked up sharply, seeing Lord Whitaker grinning.

"The ball we have just now departed from," he continued, looking at Andrew as though he expected him to be pleased. "Lady Henrietta was there only half an hour ago, and I am certain that she will linger there still. Shall we all make our way there now?"

"A capital idea!" Lord Dorchester exclaimed as Andrew's heart began to pound furiously. "I am sure that no one will mind if we all step in for a short while."

"I am certain they will not, for it is Lord Gillingham's ball, and he is always delighted to receive additional company," Lord Rushford agreed, gesturing to Andrew to stand up. "Come then, let us see if–"

"Wait!" Lord Arthington was the one to speak and Andrew breathed out a slow sigh of relief, sure that his friend was now to come to his aid. "It is a little unfair to step out in such a way when–"

"Yes, indeed it is!" Andrew exclaimed, his fingers curling a little more tightly around his glass. "I should say so."

Lord Arthington sent him a small, sideways glance and then cleared his throat.

"Apologies. What I was going to say was that I thought it a little unfair to make our way to Lord Gillingham's ball without first setting the bet. What are the consequences to be for either gentleman?"

Andrew closed his eyes and groaned aloud. He had thought Lord Arthington was to help him, but now it seemed his friend was enjoying the prospect of a bet just as much as every other man there.

"If you are wrong, then you must pay a certain amount," Lord Whitaker exclaimed, though this was immediately refused by Lord Rushford.

"Money means very little to Lord Wileham," he said, though Andrew could not entirely disagree. "It will not be troublesome to him."

Rising from his chair, Andrew looked Lord Rushford full in the face, choosing not to back away from this bet nor be truthful and tell him that he did not think he would be able to recognize Lady Henrietta after all. It was foolish, yes, but Andrew was not about to lose face now. Somehow, he would find a way to recognize Lady Henrietta before it was demanded of him, and thus, win the bet.

"What is it that you think would trouble me, then?" he asked, as Lord Rushford narrowed his eyes. "This is all utter nonsense, Rushford. Why you are making such a fuss about one lady simply because she is a relative of yours is quite beyond me."

Lord Rushford smiled suddenly, his expression changing from one of darkness to mirth.

"I have it. You will have to focus all of your attention on *one* lady – a lady of my choosing – and instead of throwing mere flirtations at her, you will have to take tea with her, walk with her, dance with her on *more* than one occasion and the like and–"

"It should be Lady Carsington!"

Andrew's eyes closed tightly as Lord Arthington's voice rang out across the room, a stabbing pain lancing through his heart.

"She is not inclined towards Wileham in the least, and he has been fretting over some ridiculous embarrassment and thus–"

"That is quite enough, Arthington." Spinning around, Andrew glared at his friend and saw the man shrink back. "Pray do not speak any further."

Lord Arthington frowned, then ran one hand over his eyes.

"My apologies," he murmured, now appearing a little abashed. "The liquor has loosened my tongue."

"So it seems."

When he looked back at Lord Rushford, however, the gentleman was grinning broadly, his arms folded lightly across his chest.

"Lady Carsington, then," he said, firmly. "You will focus all of your attentions on her, should you fail to win this bet."

"And for you?" Andrew asked, puffing out his chest a little in defiance. "What shall I say for you?"

"Say whatever you wish." Lord Rushford's grin did not fade even a little. "You are set to lose this bet, Wileham. You may speak confidently and walk about with assurance in your steps, but I can see in your eyes that, on this occasion, it is nothing but falsehood. So say whatever you wish and let us take our leave. We will see who wins this particular bet... and I believe that the favor already lies with me."

~

"I DO APOLOGIZE, WILEHAM."

Andrew coughed gruffly and settled his face into a frown.

"I do not know what you were thinking, Arthington."

"I was *not* thinking, which is precisely the problem," his friend replied, as they walked into Lord Gillingham's ballroom. "What can I do by way of apology?"

"You can tell me who Lady Henrietta is." Looking at Lord Arthington, Andrew caught his friend's widened eyes. "In truth, I do not recall at all as to who she might be."

Lord Arthington winced.

"I am not certain I can be of much aid to you. I do not know the lady very well."

"But you do know her," Andrew put in. "What color of hair does she have? Are her eyes green or brown? Are–"

"Blue, I think," Lord Arthington said, quickly. "And with very dark hair."

Andrew blinked, taken aback by his friend's sudden change in attitude.

"You do recall her, then?"

"I think it is she I am thinking of."

This was not the most encouraging answer Andrew could have been given, but as it was the only help he was going to have, he could not complain about it.

"Very well. A lady with dark hair and blue eyes."

For a moment, his thoughts returned to Lady Carsington, recalling how her hair had shone like copper on their last, most recent meeting and how her eyes had been so very cold when he had asked her to join him on a carriage ride. Why that desire had come to him -and where precisely it had come from – Andrew could not say and even now, the memory of it was more than a little mortifying. How grateful he was that his friends could not see into his thoughts for, if they could, then he would be all the more embarrassed.

Which is why I must identify Lady Henrietta correctly, he reminded himself. *I do not want to encourage this strange feeling within myself as regards Lady Carsington.*

"Very well, then!" Lord Rushford stepped back and put one hand on Andrew's shoulder. "There, do you see? There are a cluster of five ladies to the right of the mistletoe bough." Andrew nodded, his stomach dropping low as he identified not one but two ladies with dark brown hair and from where they stood, he was much too far away to know whether their eyes were blue or not. "One of them is Lady Henrietta, my cousin – and the one who thinks herself drawn to you. Which one is she?"

The smile which spread across Lord Rushford's face was not a particularly pleasant one, and the hair stood up on the back of Andrew's neck. A little helpless, he gestured to them.

"They are all so very far away. How am I to be able to tell one face from another?"

"That is no excuse!" Lord Rushford exclaimed, only for Lord Arthington to come to Andrew's defense, stating that they ought to move a little closer.

After some further reluctance on Lord Rushford's part, the gentlemen moved across the room a little more and, as they did so, the group of five ladies all glanced in their direction.

Keeping his gaze fixed upon one with dark hair, Andrew tried to ascertain the color of her eyes but found he could not. The second, however, he was sure had blue eyes and if Lord Arthington was correct, then the lady in question had dark hair and blue eyes, which made *this* one none other than Lady Henrietta.

"There." His chin lifted and he smiled with a confidence he did not truly feel. "The young lady in question is standing to the very front of the group of ladies, with her dark hair and green gown which, no doubt, highlights the blue of her eyes."

There was a silence and as Andrew turned to look at Lord Rushford, the broad smile splitting the gentleman's face gave him his answer.

He had failed. The bet was lost – and now he had no other choice but to deal with the consequences.

CHAPTER SIX

*J*ulianna smiled and set her teacup down on the saucer again.

"Thank you for coming to call, Marianne. I must admit, I did not even *think* of putting up the greenery in the house until you came to call!"

Lady Gilford laughed, her eyes twinkling.

"I hope you did not think that I overstepped?"

With her smile growing even more, Julianna shook her head, turning her gaze in the direction of the table where a large pile of holly, small pine branches, tendrils of ivy and other greenery now sat, combined with ribbons and other colorful pieces. Lady Gilford had brought it with her, the footmen carrying it in from the carriage, telling Julianna that she had ordered *far* too much for her own townhouse and prayed that Julianna could use the excess to decorate her own home.

"Now, tell me about Lord Wileham," Lady Gilford continued, pulling Julianna away from the greenery. "He has been paying you a great deal of attention, has he not?"

"I should hardly say a great deal!" Julianna exclaimed, a

little concerned at her friend's remarks. "He has asked me to dance on two occasions, though I refused the second. That is all."

"And he asked you to take a ride in his carriage with him, did he not?"

"Which I *also* refused," Julianna stated, firmly. "I was not about to permit him to treat me as he has done every other young lady of his acquaintance! I have been forewarned, and thus I was more than ready to refuse him."

"Though it is strange," Lady Gilford remarked, picking up her teacup again. "He is not a gentleman who has *ever* requested that a lady join him in his carriage, and I am a little surprised to hear that he did such a thing!"

A swell rose in her stomach and Julianna fought back the sensation, trying to remain as calm and as indifferent about Lord Wileham as she could – outwardly, at least.

"Perhaps he is aware of my lack of interest in him."

"Perhaps." Lady Gilford sighed, then rose to her feet. "And alas, though I should very much like to stay longer, I must take my leave. My dear husband has requested that I return home to make sure our invitations for the Christmas ball are quite ready. You are going to join us, are you not?"

Julianna smiled and rose also.

"I should be glad to join you on any occasion to which you seek to invite me, Marianne."

"Excellent." Lady Gilford kissed her lightly on the cheek then grasped her hands. "Then you will join us for Christmas Day, I hope? Lord and Lady Thurston are to join us also, and Laura and I would be so delighted if you were present."

Julianna squeezed her friend's hands.

"You are very kind to think of inviting me."

"Then you will come? I could not bear to think of you

sitting here alone, and Christmas Day is only a few weeks away now, so plans must be made!"

Laughing softly at her friend's enthusiasm, Julianna nodded.

"Yes, of course. I would be glad to accept. I thank you."

"How wonderful."

With a few words of farewell and a promise that they would see each other again that evening at Lord St. Madoes' soiree, Lady Gilford took her farewell, and left Julianna entirely alone.

With a small sigh and a smile on her face, Julianna wandered back towards the table and let her fingers trail along the green ivy.

Her heart began to ache, and her smile began to crack, recalling how she had spent the last few Christmases with nothing but loneliness and sorrow in her heart. Yes, she had been with friends, but it did not take away from the fact that she had returned to an empty house at the end of the day. It would be the same again this year, but perhaps, now that she was back in London, it would not be as painful. Thus far, the wider company, the many occasions and the rekindled friendships had brought her a good deal of happiness, the likes of which she had not felt in some time.

"Lord Wileham, my Lady."

Starting in surprise, Julianna turned to see her butler stepping from the room, no doubt intending to go and make sure that a fresh tray of tea and cakes was sent up immediately. Lord Wileham was bowing and, sinking into a curtsey, Julianna gave herself a few minutes to regain her composure, both startled by his arrival, and by her own reaction to his presence.

"Lord Wileham." Her throat was a little tight and she

cleared it quickly, her heart still pounding in her chest. "Good afternoon."

"Good afternoon. I do hope that I am not intruding?"

"No, not at all."

She glanced around, noting with relief that the maid had come to sit in the corner of the room without her bidding – no doubt at the request of her butler. She must remember to thank him later. While there was nothing overly improper about a widow having a gentleman coming to call, it would be better if there was a maid present, even if it only served to quieten the servants' wagging tongues! All the same, Julianna herself felt unease clawing at her heart while the pull of his eyes upon hers was something she fought hard to ignore, keeping her gaze near the floor instead.

"Were you intending to do something with this?" he asked, giving her no indication about why he had come to call upon her. "It has been some time since I have had anything to do with decorating the house for Christmas. Normally, I leave it to the servants."

"I see." Did he realize that he sounded dismissive, as though the greenery on the table was something to be brushed aside as insignificant? "I was intending to make a few wreaths, in fact," she continued, making her way towards the table as a stab of indignation over his remark filled her. "It takes some skill, however, so I am not at all surprised that you leave such things to your servants."

This seemed to needle him, for he drew himself up at once, his swirling green eyes flashing.

"I am certain that I would be able to do it."

"Very well." Emboldened, she gestured to a chair, and sat down on one herself. "Come then."

Lord Wileham blinked, then put his hands on the back of the chair rather than sitting down in it.

"I beg your pardon?"

"If you believe that you could make a wreath, then why do you not sit down and do so?"

There must have been a challenge in her expression – for she certainly heard it in her voice – for Lord Wileham's jaw tightened, and he rounded the chair before sitting down with a thump.

"Very well. What am I to do first?"

"First, you must select what you wish to use in your wreath," she stated calmly, gesturing to the array on the table. "Though you must take care."

Lord Wileham scowled.

"I do not think that – ouch!"

Julianna fought to hide her smile. Lord Wileham had reached out and taken hold of a piece of holly and, as it seemed that he had not realized that it was sharp, was now nursing a cut to his thumb.

"You must take care because it is sharp," she finished, as Lord Wileham pulled out a handkerchief and wrapped it around his thumb, still scowling. "Now, if you are not too injured, then I shall show you the next part."

The butler came up with tea at that very moment and Julianna directed him to put it between herself and Lord Wileham. Soon, she was busy directing Lord Wileham in the process of making his wreath and, much to her surprise, the scowl quickly left his face as he wove ivy in and out, adding a curled ribbon here, and a cluster of red holly berries there.

She allowed herself to study him, her own wreath being now almost finished, given that she had made them many a time before. Lord Wileham was concentrating most severely, his brow furrowed, and his mouth pinched, but there was a steadiness in his eyes which she had not seen before. He was concentrating entirely on the task, not permitting himself to be distracted by anything or anyone else, and she had to admit that her attraction towards him intensified. She had always admitted that he was handsome, but now, his dark hair falling over his forehead, his lip caught between his teeth, and the gentleness of his hands on the greenery, he was all the more so. This was Lord Wileham as she had never seen him before and the smile on his face when he lifted the wreath to admire it made her heart thunder in her chest.

Then he winced.

"In comparison with yours, Lady Carsington, I do not think that I have done particularly well!"

"But it is only your first attempt," she said, in what she hoped was an encouraging manner. "And I think it looks very good."

His eyes caught hers.

"Truly?"

The smile on her face was genuine, her heart softening towards him, despite her attempts to remain as indifferent to him as she could.

"Truly, Lord Wileham. I would not lie to you. I think that the wreath will look very well on one of the walls in your house."

"Oh, I shall not take it home with me!" he exclaimed, setting it on the table between them. "You must keep it here. I have no decorations in my house as yet and I do not think–"

"Please take it." The softness of her voice broke Lord Wileham's protestations. "I think it is something you ought to be proud of."

Lord Wileham hesitated, then smiled.

"It shall remind me to listen to you before I place my hand into a pile of greenery," he remarked, holding up his thumb and making her laugh, though his soiled handkerchief had been taken by the butler so that it could be washed, cleaned, and returned to Lord Wileham as soon as was possible. "Thank you, Lady Carsington. This was a good deal more enjoyable than I had anticipated."

"I am glad to hear it."

For a long moment, they simply looked at each other across the table and, though Julianna's heart began to pound, she could think of nothing to say, nothing with which to fill the silence... and yet, she realized, she did not wish to. Simply looking at him was enough. This afternoon had shown her another side to Lord Wileham, perhaps a hint of his true self, rather than the flirtatious, coy gentleman who wanted nothing more than to capture the attention of as many young ladies as he could, without ever returning their interest in any way.

"A carriage ride, Lady Carsington?"

She blinked, hearing the hoarseness in Lord Wileham's voice.

"I have asked you to join me once already, I know, and you were not inclined towards it," he continued, before she had a chance to reply. "But I have been given the assurance that we will have a good many blankets and hot bricks and as much as can be done as possible to ensure your comfort. And if that is not to your liking, then mayhap you might consent to walk with me, as you have agreed to do with Lord Pleasanton?"

Words of consent were on her lips in an instant, but Julianna clamped her mouth shut, dropped her gaze to her lap and clasped her fingers tightly together.

"Might I ask why, Lord Wileham?"

Darting a gaze up towards him, she saw him frown and her heart sank low. What was his reason for his eagerness for her company? She would not permit herself to think that it might be because he had a genuine interest in being with her, for after what Lady Gilford and Lady Thurston had said to her of him, she understood precisely the sort of gentleman he was – one who sought his own pleasures and nothing more.

Lord Wileham spread his hands and let out a hiss of breath.

"Must I explain why a gentleman might wish to linger in the company of a lady?"

His question hung between them, and Julianna frowned, seeing that he had not answered her own question at all. Instead, he had pushed it aside and asked a question of his own, rather than be truthful with her.

Then I must be bold.

"You wish to further your acquaintance with me?" When he nodded, she took another deep breath, but forced the words from her lips. "For what end?"

Lord Wileham blinked slowly, cat like, mayhap considering his answer which, again, gave Julianna a good deal of concern as to his true intentions.

"I should not have... forgive me, Lady Carsington."

Her brows dropped low.

"Forgive you?"

"I should have thought to ask. Some of those who are widowed seek to remain so. I ought not to have presumed that you might be eager for a closer connection with another gentleman."

Julianna went hot all over, her face burning as she pulled her eyes away from him, her stomach lurching. Was it true, then? Was he seeking to further his acquaintance with her in the hope of a deeper connection? Of courtship, perhaps engagement and marriage?

"I had not considered…"

"Forgive me."

He rose and then bowed.

"I shall take my leave. I –"

"I should like to go for a walk with you, Lord Wileham."

Her endless attempts at keeping hold of her tongue had now suddenly smashed into shattered pieces. Lord Wileham's eyes flared and then he smiled.

"Excellent. Thank you, Lady Carsington. I am truly honored by your willingness to walk with me."

"It – it will have to be brief, given the weather." Frustrated at her own swiftness, her own eagerness, she restrained herself as best she could. "I do not think I could bear to get too cold, even though walking through the snow can be very lovely indeed."

"I quite understand." He bowed again, a smile still lingering on his lips. "I shall send a note, detailing the day and the time." Picking up his wreath, he held it out again, his eyes fixed on it and a softness coming about his lips, as if he were truly delighted with all that had happened between them that afternoon. "Good afternoon, Lady Carsington."

"Good afternoon."

Letting her eyes follow him, Julianna took a slow breath and then released it, her shoulders relaxing as a mixture of excitement and regret swarmed together within her.

Just what had she done?

CHAPTER SEVEN

"And how do you fare with Lady Carsington?"

Andrew grimaced.

"I do not know what your intention was in setting that bet, Dorchester, but I do not appreciate it."

Lord Dorchester smirked.

"It is just a little fun, that is all."

"But you are doing it specifically to irritate me," Andrew responded, watching his friend with careful eyes. "What is it that I have done to encourage such disdain? And no, you need not pretend that it is nothing of any importance, I can tell that you are disinclined towards me at present."

A dark smile crossed Lord Dorchester's face, his eyebrows knotting and a shadow in his eyes.

"It should not surprise me that you remain unaware of what it is you did, despite the fact that you promised me you would not."

"I would not do what?"

"Precisely." Lord Dorchester rolled his eyes and sighed. "I did ask you specifically to stay away from Miss Sophia

Hallstrom, did I not?"

Andrew swallowed hard, his eyes closing for a moment.

"Yes, you did."

"But you did not."

A thousand excuses sprang to his lips – he had forgotten, he had not known who the lady was, it had only been a dance and a few short conversations... but he refused to say a single word of an excuse.

"No, Dorchester, I did not."

"And such is the extent of our friendship, such is the closeness between you and I, that you did not even *remember* what I had asked you, despite your statement that you wished to support me in this new venture towards courtship and betrothal to the lady."

There was a twist of anger running through Lord Dorchester's voice, and when Andrew looked at his friend, he caught the tightness about his jaw and saw how his hands clenched tightly.

"I have injured you. I am sorry."

A hard laugh snapped from Lord Dorchester's throat.

"You have not injured me. You have shown me the truth about your character and, to be frank, it is not something which I find myself respectful of, in any way. Indeed, I begin to wonder why we are friends, given how poorly you have treated my request."

At this, Andrew's heart began to quicken as shame grew like a great and heavy cloud which sat above his head.

"Pray, do not think that I do not have consideration for you, Dorchester," he said, though his friend shook his head. "I made a mistake – a grave mistake, certainly, but I did not do so deliberately."

"You say such a thing, but I believe that a person's actions show their character more than their mere words."

Andrew took in a long breath and put out one hand towards the other guests, letting his gaze run over them.

"I was distracted, Dorchester, that is all," he said, as his friend snorted. "You know very well what I am – a gentleman who has no intention of matrimony and yet who enjoys the brief company of the ladies of London. You were that way yourself for many a year."

"Yes, I was." Lord Dorchester scowled. "But I have changed. I have realized the selfishness behind my actions, the self-absorption which covered everything else, and I have come to regret living in such a way. This new path I am walking goes in the opposite direction, and does not weave its way alongside yours, Wileham."

Andrew did not know what to say. The cloying shame sent a lump into his throat, pushing away any words of excuse as he began to realize just how deeply he had hurt Lord Dorchester. Even now, he did not recall stepping out with Miss Hallstrom, dancing with her or even conversing with her, for she had only been one face among many - but Lord Dorchester was quite right to be angry with him for his lack of regard. He ought to have taken a good deal more care, ought to have actually considered who he was stepping out with, and recalled his promise to Lord Dorchester. Instead, he had done nothing of the sort, and had focused entirely on himself, just as he had always done.

"I will think on what you have said," Andrew said, somewhat humbly which garnered a look of surprise from Lord Dorchester. "I truly did not mean to cause you pain. It was unintentionally done, but I can see that yes, I ought to have been a good deal more careful than I was. I should have remembered what you had asked of me."

"Yes. You should have done all of those things – but you did not."

"And so you sought to punish me for my inconsideration, by placing a consequence upon my head."

"A consequence you brought upon yourself – though there is benefit for me also. You will not be *permitted* to toy with any other young lady save for Lady Carsington, which protects Miss Hallstrom from you, regardless," Lord Dorchester stated, swinging around to face Andrew again, his eyes a little narrowed now, one finger pointing straight at Andrew's chest. "All you needed to do was tell Lord Rushford that you did not recall Lady Henrietta, and all would have been well. He might have been a little irritated, but to take it as far as a bet – knowing that you would lose – was both courageous and ridiculous."

Andrew dropped his head.

"I thought I would be able to recall her when I saw her."

"When are you ever going to change?" Lord Dorchester threw up his hands, then let them fall to his sides. "Do you not see that this manner of things, this continual focus on the ladies of the *ton,* your desire to fleetingly know each one, and have them think well of you, means that you do not get to experience any true happiness?"

"And you think that you have found true happiness?"

A little surprised at how sharply the words came from his mouth, Andrew twisted his lips together so that he could not say more, looking out at the rest of the room, rather than at Lord Dorchester. There came a short pause, but Andrew dared not glance over at him again, praying silently that he had not made things worse.

"I do not know if I have found true happiness as yet." Lord Dorchester spoke slowly, giving great consideration to each of his words. "I cannot say, for I do not know the lady well enough yet. From what has begun to grow between us, however, I *can* say that I am a good deal more contented than I was before. My eyes are drawn only to her, my smile is brought about simply because she is near."

The quietness of his voice had Andrew looking at his friend again, somewhat confused by the change in his temperament.

"I think, Wileham, that there is more to be said for a young lady being the single focus for a gentleman than you might ever have considered." Lord Dorchester took a breath and then released it again, smiling quietly to himself, as though he held some great secret close to himself. "Perhaps you will find it yourself, now that you are forced into this situation with Lady Carsington – though I will admit that was not specifically my desire when the idea first came to mind!"

Andrew swallowed hard, coughing to clear his throat while feeling an uncomforting prickling running up his spine. He did not much like what Lord Dorchester was saying, and disliked it all the more given that it was beginning to edge into his mind as something which made sense. In his last interactions with Lady Carsington, had he not found himself in a different state from his usual, erratic self? He had sat down at a table with her and made a wreath. It had been a quiet task, one where he had listened to her direction and found himself enjoying the stillness, the quiet and the company. There had not been the desire to jump around the room, to find someone else to speak with, nor to find who else he might need to draw close to. Instead, there had been a contentment – and even a joy – in making the wreath with Lady Carsington. Even now, as his thoughts went back to that afternoon, Andrew caught himself smiling – and then pushed that thought immediately aside.

I cannot permit myself to feel anything for the lady, he reminded himself, sternly. *I am the uncatchable gentleman!*

Regardless of what Lord Dorchester says, I have no intention of marrying. Not yet, at least.

Lord Dorchester cleared his throat.

"I do hope we can continue as friends. If you are genuine in what you say."

Andrew turned as Lord Dorchester arched an eyebrow, clearly uncertain whether Andrew had meant what he had said previously.

"I can assure you, I fully intend to consider what you have said and act in a far better manner than before."

"Then perhaps we shall still be able to be friends." A frown tugged at Lord Dorchester's forehead again. "Though you must promise me to stay far from Miss Hallstrom. I believe that her affection for me is genuine, but I am also aware of how many young ladies respond to you when you focus all of your attentions upon them."

Andrew put one hand to his heart.

"I give you my word, Dorchester, I will not go near the lady again. I may smile and speak amiably, but it will be nothing more than that, I assure you. I will not so much as dance with her."

Lord Dorchester relaxed visibly, his shoulders loosening and, when he smiled, it chased away the lingering shadows from his face.

"I am glad to hear that from you, Wileham." One eyebrow lifted just a little. "Now let us see if you can prove that your words and intentions are genuine."

∽

"You appear a little troubled this evening, Lord Wileham."

Andrew glanced at Lady Carsington, a little surprised by her remark.

"Do I?"

"You were long in conversation with Lord Dorchester before you came to speak with me," she said, her eyes reflecting the soft glow of the flickering candlelight. "Is all quite well?"

The edge of Andrew's lips curved.

"You were watching me, then?"

Instantly, Lady Carsington looked away, but she did not smile, as he had expected her to. Instead, she frowned, her mouth tugging to one side - and Andrew's ready smile fell away. She had asked him a question that spoke of concern and genuine interest and, instead of answering her, he had teased her and tried to make light of what she had said to him.

"Forgive me, Lady Carsington."

"You are always ready with a quick remark, are you not?" Her eyes turned back to his, but they did not glow softly as they had done only a few moments ago. Instead, they were dulled with frustration, though her face was a little flushed. "I am not about to respond in the way that you expect, Lord Wileham. I will not laugh and smile and look back at you with fluttering eyelashes. I am a widowed lady and, as such, have no interest in such flirtations."

"Forgive me."

Aware of how his heart slammed hard into his chest, his brows knotted together at his own reaction. Why was he so confused, all in a muddle, when it came to this lady?

Because she does not act in the same way as every other young lady has done when she is around me.

Yes, that was the reason, he realized. He was uncertain around her, because he did not know what she would say, how she would react, nor whether anything he did or said would make her smile. She was unlike any other young lady of his acquaintance and that, for whatever reason, was catching his attention.

"You are not yourself today, I think."

The statement held a question within it and Andrew nodded slowly, unused to sharing the truths of his heart with anyone.

"I have upset my friend."

"I see." She turned towards him a little more, her eyes searching his face. "Unintentionally?"

"Yes, unintentionally, though I do not say that I lack responsibility for it, however."

Lady Carsington nodded.

"I can understand what you mean."

"I have promised him that I will not do the same thing again, and sworn to him that I will take a good deal more care." It seemed as though, the more he spoke, the quieter the raging sea of his soul became. "The way Lord Dorchester spoke, it is as if he has discovered a great treasure and I am standing at a distance, watching him find it."

"A treasure?" Lady Carsington tilted her head a little. "What does he speak of? It cannot be coin, for I am certain that he has more than enough of that!"

Andrew could not hide his laugh, and when it broke from his lips, Lady Carsington smiled with him, her eyes twinkling.

"No, indeed it is not, Lady Carsington. He speaks of..." Uncertain as to whether he might be betraying a confidence should he speak of anything specific, he chose to be careful. "There is a young lady he finds himself drawn to."

"Ah yes, Miss Hallstrom."

Blinking in confusion, Andrew frowned, only for Lady

Carsington to laugh and put a hand on his arm.

"You need not look so concerned, Lord Wileham. It is simply what ladies do, I am afraid. We share news of such things and, I confess, though I do not know the lady nor Lord Dorchester either, I have heard that he is an... interesting fellow."

"He is a gentleman very much such as I am, who has never before considered courtship. I, however, have every intention of remaining that way, for now at least, while he appears to have changed his mind on such matters." For some reason, Lady Carsington suddenly went very pale indeed. Her eyebrows lifted, she opened her mouth and then closed it again, only to then turn her head sharply and frown hard. "I do hope I have not troubled you in some way?" A little concerned as to her rapid change in color, Andrew stepped closer and found his hand going to her arm. "Lord Dorchester is –"

"I am quite well, I thank you." Interrupting him, Lady Carsington smiled briskly, looked up at him and gave herself a small shake. "It was nothing. However, I must now step away in search of my friends, for I did promise them that I would sit to play cards with them both this evening." Bobbing quickly, she turned her head and moved away. "I will see you in two days' time for our walk, however. Good evening, Lord Wileham."

Andrew's brow furrowed as he remained silent and watchful, wondering what it was that had sent Lady Carsington practically running from his company. With a heavy breath, he shook his head and ran one hand through his hair, a little astonished to realize just how disappointed he was about her departure from his side.

Perhaps all would become clear when they walked together in the park.

CHAPTER EIGHT

"And you say that your husband has been gone some three years?"

Julianna blinked in surprise at Lord Pleasanton's question.

"Yes," she answered, a little confused as to why he would be showing this particular subject so much interest. "Three years."

"That must be very difficult for you." Lord Pleasanton turned to look at her before resuming his walk by her side. "Three years alone is no pleasant thing."

"It has been trying, but I have been blessed by companions and friends who have drawn close to me."

"Mmm." Lord Pleasanton said nothing for some minutes, and Julianna tried to keep the frown from her face, wondering if she could find something to say that might take them away from the subject of her late husband. Thus far, her walk with Lord Pleasanton had not been particularly enjoyable, though it was not because she disliked the cold. Rather, his company was proving somewhat difficult for, thus far, all he had spoken about was her widowed state and her late husband. "And you say that you are not living at your late husband's estate?"

"No." Julianna glanced at him again, noting how the gentleman rubbed at his chin. "My late husband's brother, the new Lord Carsington, has now taken on the title. He did not cast me from the estate, however, but rather insisted that I stay as long as I wished."

"And where is it that you reside now?"

Julianna closed her eyes briefly.

"I have a small house left to me in my late husband's will."

She did not say anything more, did not say a word about the will, or the house itself, nor even about her inheritance, growing concerned that the only reason Lord Pleasanton was asking her such questions was because he needed to ascertain some things about her before he could continue with their acquaintance. Was he impoverished? Or simply eager to know what financial implications it might have if he continued with their relationship, such as it was.

"And you are to stay in London for the Christmas Season. Do you intend to return home after that, or linger in London until the Season itself begins?"

"I do intend to stay." This had not really been a consideration, not until this moment, but the questions Lord Pleasanton was putting to her demanded immediate answers. "I may change my mind, however."

"Why would you do so?"

Julianna frowned, wondering if his questions were leading her to a path which she did not necessarily want to walk on.

"It is my prerogative, I suppose," she answered, carefully. "I have no husband, no one waiting desperately for my return. If I decided to go back home after all, I think I would then return for some of the London Season, though that itself seems so very far away."

"Why, it is only a few months!" Lord Pleasanton grinned at her, and Julianna managed a smile, for what was the first time since they had started walking together. "But tell me, do you have intentions to marry again, Lady Carsington?"

The shock of his spectacularly forward question caught Julianna unawares and her breath hitched, her feet stumbling a little. Lord Pleasanton caught her arm and then chuckled, slipping it through his own so that she had no choice but to walk alongside him. The boldness of not only his questions, but also his actions towards her, had Julianna's heart pounding as her instinct to escape him grew suddenly fierce.

"Alas, Lord Pleasanton," she said, trying to pull her arm away from his, but failing spectacularly given the strength of his frame, "I fear that such a question is one that a gentleman such as yourself ought not to ask! It is rather rude, do you not think?"

"Rude?" Lord Pleasanton shook his head. "No, I do not think so, not if there is to be a connection between us."

Julianna's heart dropped, her stomach swirling with waves of anxiety.

"A connection?"

"Yes." Lord Pleasanton smiled at her, then looked back to the path as though what he was saying was just as she ought to have expected. "My dear Lady Carsington, you have been wed before, so I am sure that you understand the ways of gentlemen. You know that we are required to marry and produce an heir and thus, being a gentleman with a title and an estate, that is precisely what I intend to do - which is why, of course, I invited you out to walk with me. I am sure that my interest in you cannot have been too hidden, since I was so obvious in my attentions!"

Slowing her steps in an attempt to have Lord Pleasanton release her arm, Julianna shook her head, looking up at him steadily.

"Lord Pleasanton, please understand me when I say to you that I have no interest whatsoever in becoming your wife. I had not thought that a walk in the park would signify so much!"

A line pulled between his brows.

"But you accepted."

"Yes, but that does not mean that I am then willing to step into church with you."

Lord Pleasanton's expression grew ugly, his jaw tight, his mouth pulling down as he finally let go of her arm.

"I do not think you can say such things with any authenticity, Lady Carsington. As I have said, you have been wed before and –"

"My late husband did not think that one quiet walk through the park was the promise of betrothal, Lord Pleasanton!"

Lord Pleasanton threw up his hands, his face hot despite the cold air which ran between them.

"You need not attempt to compare me to your late husband, Lady Carsington! I have no doubt that he and I are very different gentlemen, with differing ways of going about such things. However, my intention for you remains the same."

Julianna closed her eyes, flames licking up into her cheeks.

"And *my* intentions remain clear," she stated firmly, opening her eyes to gaze back up into his face, her hands clenched by her sides. "Should you ask me to consider courtship, then I have every intention of refusing."

"Then you are ridiculous," Lord Pleasanton stated, with all the air of an aggrieved gentleman who believed he was still quite in the right about everything. "You are a widow, Lady Carsington. Do you really believe you will be given many offers of marriage?" Laughing harshly, he leaned closer, his eyes shifting into narrowness. "I can assure you, they will be few and far between. You may have property, a small fortune, and a fine character, but that does not take away from the fact that you have already been wife to another gentleman."

Tears pricked in Julianna's eyes as she looked at Lord Pleasanton, though whether it was anger or pain which forced them to her eyes, she could not say. Her breathing was ragged, and her nails bit into her palms, but she accepted the pain, using it to try to steady herself.

"Might I enquire if everything is quite all right?"

A voice she had not expected to hear, and yet was delighted to recognize as Lord Wileham's, came between her and Lord Pleasanton and, turning in that direction, Julianna swallowed and looked straight back into his eyes. The last time she had seen him was two days prior, when he had mentioned, off-hand, that he had no intention of wedding, and she had found her heart aching with such a sharp pain, that the only thing she could do to lessen the pain was to walk away.

"Lady Carsington?"

Seeing him waiting for her answer, Julianna took a breath and gestured to Lord Pleasanton.

"I am afraid that Lord Pleasanton's company is a little less than what would be desired," she answered, though Lord Pleasanton rolled his eyes. "Lord Pleasanton was telling me all of the reasons why I would not be suitable as a wife while, at the same time, expecting me to make my way to church with him very soon indeed!"

Lord Wileham's eyebrows lifted significantly, though Lord Pleasanton did not look away.

"And what reasons were these, might I ask?" he said, though Lord Pleasanton only shrugged. "You will not tell me, Lord Pleasanton? Then, no doubt, they were nothing but nonsense."

Julianna drew herself up.

"They were indeed."

"I think that any gentleman would be glad to stand up with Lady Carsington," Lord Wileham declared, surprising Julianna with his vehemence. "Your words were clearly not spoken kindly. I think that you owe the lady an apology."

Lord Pleasanton snorted, obviously not taking well to what Lord Wileham had said, nor to Julianna's prior statements.

"I think I shall take my leave. It seems that we are *not* to be bound together, as I had hoped, Lady Carsington. Good afternoon."

Julianna did not utter a single word, did not make even a single sound as she watched Lord Pleasanton make his way back along the path which led to his carriage, only for her to then let out a yelp of dismay.

"What is it?"

Lord Wileham's eyes went wide, and Julianna closed hers briefly, frustrated now.

"Lord Pleasanton took me from my townhouse," she explained, sighing as she opened her eyes to watch his retreating figure. "I shall have to hail a hackney."

"Or you can permit me to take you home," Lord Wileham suggested, a smile on his face now, though when he glanced in Lord Pleasanton's direction, the smile quickly fell away. "I do not understand the detail of what you were discussing, but he has certainly not left a pleasing impression of himself!"

Julianna did not say what was on her mind, for it immediately came to her that Lord Wileham had not left her with the most favorable initial impression either only for her then to consider the time they had spent together of late, which had been much more pleasant.

"Will you consent to sit in my carriage so I might have my driver take you home?"

The quietness of his voice, the way his eyes searched hers, took Julianna a little by surprise. He was not teasing her, was not making any coy remarks about sitting in a carriage together but was, instead, simply asking her in a very general manner whether she would accept or not.

There was no question of her answer.

"Yes, Lord Wileham. I think I would be glad to, although..." Biting her lip, she hesitated for a moment. "Might I ask if you would be willing to walk with me for a few minutes? I know it is very cold, and the snow is threatening to fall, but I confess myself to be a little overcome by various emotions after what Lord Pleasanton has said to me just now."

Lord Wileham nodded as if he understood.

"And walking will relieve you of such feelings?"

"Perhaps a little," she answered with a wry smile. "I shall simply ruminate on it otherwise."

"Then I consent at once!" he agreed, stepping beside her, but not offering his arm, as she thought he might do. "We were due to take our walk together tomorrow, but it seems as though we are to have it today after all."

"Yes, it seems we are," she agreed, softly, looking up at

him as he clasped his hands behind his back, his face turned towards hers. "Did you intentionally come here for a walk at the same time as I was to be here with Lord Pleasanton?"

Lord Wileham looked away at once.

"Forgive me, it must appear as though I planned to be in the park at the same time, but I can assure you, that was not my intention."

Realizing that she must have sounded a little accusatory, Julianna smiled quickly and put her hand on his arm for just a moment.

"I do not mean anything by it. I only meant to ask if you were eager for a short walk in the fresh air this afternoon."

"Oh." Lord Wileham's face cleared as he smiled. "Then yes, that is precisely what I wanted. A space to clear the thoughts from my head so I might concentrate on other matters a good deal more carefully."

Julianna smiled, understanding the concept of having her head so full of tumbling thoughts, it could barely be contained. She had been wondering exactly why she had responded with such upset upon hearing that Lord Wileham had no intention of marriage and, even now, as she looked into his eyes, Julianna struggled to find any reason other than the fact that she liked the gentleman.

Which was ridiculous, of course.

"For what it is worth, Lady Carsington, I do not think that there is any reason that any gentleman in all of London might think of you in a poor light."

She looked at him, catching the soft shimmer about his eyes and noticing how gentle flakes of snow were beginning to fall all around them. Another glance around the park and Julianna's heart quickened, realizing that they were the only two out in the park now. Everyone else – though there had only been a few – seemed to have already taken their leave, perhaps chased away by the threatening snow cloud.

"You are very kind, Lord Wileham."

His laugh was not one that she had expected, nor was the rueful smile which danced about his lips.

"No, Lady Carsington, I am not a kind man. The truth is, I believe that I have been a very self-absorbed, unkind fellow for some time. Though now, perhaps, I am considering whether I wish to continue on that path."

"I think that there is some goodness in you," she said, surprising herself with how fervently she spoke. "I confess that I do not know you particularly well as yet, Lord Wileham, but I have seen you make a wreath – albeit with a painful thumb – and that takes gentleness and care. And now, you have come to my aid *and* to my defense, which has left Lord Pleasanton in an unfavorable position, and pushed you forward into the light."

This did not seem to bolster Lord Wileham in any way, for he dropped his head and tore his gaze away from her, lifting one hand to rub over his eyes for a moment, a hiss of breath escaping him.

"It is a strange place to be," he remarked, when he finally lifted his head to look at her, a flush in his cheeks and his eyes darting to her face and away again. "I am not accustomed to anyone thinking particularly highly of me. I have not cared about their considerations before now... though perhaps that is mostly to do with the fact that it is *your* opinion which is being offered to me. For whatever reason, I find myself eager to improve myself in your eyes, Lady Carsington."

Julianna did not know what to say to this. Her stomach swirled, a gentle heat spiraling through her, and even though there was a low warning in the back of her thoughts, she did not hesitate when he offered her his arm. Yes, she had no real idea if this was a ploy of his, whether he wished for her to admire him and desire him as every other young lady did, or if it came from a genuine desire to do everything that he had said – but in this moment, Julianna did not care. All she wanted was to walk alongside Lord Wileham through the gently falling snow and allow herself a sense of peace and contentment as he led her back towards his carriage. There was something between them, she could no longer hide that from herself, but whether it would come to anything of consequence, Julianna did not yet dare to even imagine.

CHAPTER NINE

"So *that* is Miss Hallstrom."

Lord Arthington eyed Andrew carefully before he answered.

"Yes, it is. Lord Dorchester told me of his conversation with you."

"Did he now?" Andrew sighed inwardly, waiting for Lord Arthington to make some sort of remark, but his friend remained unusually silent. "Yes, Lord Dorchester pointed out my mistakes and my faults and I have apologized to him profusely for what I did... though I am sure that I only danced and laughed with her a little."

With a snort, Lord Arthington rolled his eyes.

"My dear friend, you know very well that your trifling and toying with the young ladies of the *ton* makes them fall head over heels in love with you, for you give them hope that *they* will be the one to catch the uncatchable gentleman. It is most frustrating to those of us who must work a little harder to get what we desire."

At this, Andrew's brows fell.

"I do not seduce them, Arthington, as well you know. If

you wish to have such liaisons, then that must be on your conscience, but do not think that my flirtations are in any way akin to your own connections."

Lord Arthington shrugged, clearly caring rather little about his own behavior. It suited him well enough, but it was not something which Andrew would ever permit for himself. To garner smiles was one thing, but to have liaisons was quite another.

"As regards Miss Hallstrom, however, I have promised Lord Dorchester that I shall barely speak a word to her," Andrew continued, eager now to move the conversation on. "I mean to do exactly as I have promised, however, so you need not give me that sharp-eyed look! The only reason I have already failed is simply because I did not recall the young lady's name."

"But now you do."

Andrew nodded.

"And this is only because you have lost your bet, I suppose."

Opening his mouth to refute this, Andrew paused for a moment and then answered.

"There is some truth in that, I think. Yes, I have lost a bet, and must now concentrate my attentions upon Lady Carsington – and with Lord Dorchester, Lord Whitaker and Lord Rushford watching me at every occasion that I attend, they shall make certain that I do not fail in that regard – but I have also had time to think upon what Lord Dorchester himself said to me, and that has given me a good deal to consider."

"Oh?"

Andrew lifted his shoulders, then let them fall.

"Mayhap the state of my character requires some consideration."

Lord Arthington blinked, his ready smile suddenly gone.

"You mean to say that you intend to follow Lord Dorchester's lead and consider matrimony?"

Laughing quickly, Andrew caught the look of relief which passed over Lord Arthington's face, though Arthington hid it hurriedly.

"No, I have no intention to wed as yet, but I *shall*, I think, consider whether what I have done these last two Seasons is worth continuing. I have been garnering the attention of every young lady I can, simply so that I might build something of a reputation for myself and then revel in it." The words were putrid on his tongue, and he spat them out, a solemnity falling over him now. "I do not think that I wish to be such a fellow any longer."

"Then permit me to take your place!" Lord Arthington's easy manner made Andrew smile, though he felt a slight sting with it. His friend did not understand, and Lord Dorchester was suspicious of him still. Who then, could he speak to, openly, about it all?

His thoughts immediately went to Lady Carsington, though why she should return to his mind at this present moment, Andrew was not entirely certain. It could not be that *she* would be the best one to share such trials with, surely? Recalling how they had enjoyed a pleasant walk together some two days ago, and then had taken tea together only yesterday - in lieu of their planned walk as he had already shared one with her - Andrew let himself smile, a soft sense of contentment in his soul. Lady Carsington was beginning to make an impression upon his heart, and he was finally willing to let her do so.

"Why are you smiling?" Lord Arthington caught his

breath, his eyes widening. "Goodness, it cannot be that you are thinking of Lady Carsington, can it?"

Andrew blinked rapidly, then shook his head.

"No, of course not."

"You *are* thinking of her!" Lord Arthington put one hand to his heart. "Pray do not tell me that you have enjoyed spending time with her thus far? This was meant to be a consequence for you, not something that you would enjoy!"

With what he hoped was a wry smile, Andrew rolled his eyes at his friend.

"My dear fellow, please do not think for a *moment* that I am at all interested in furthering my acquaintance with Lady Carsington. I can assure you, the situation is quite the opposite."

"Is that so?"

The voice which came from behind him had him turning swiftly, only to look into the face of the very person he had been speaking about. Lady Carsington's face was paling, even as he watched, though her hands were at her hips and her chin lifted.

"Lady Carsington." Stammering a little, Andrew tried desperately to find a way to explain himself but with Lady Carsington on one side and Lord Arthington on the other, he struggled desperately. "Th... that is, what I mean to say is that —"

"You have no intention of furthering your acquaintance with me," she interrupted, her eyes flashing now. "I must wonder, then, why it is that you wished to walk with me in the park, and why you insisted that we dance together, Lord Wileham, for if it is truly that you have no desire whatsoever to improve our acquaintance, then for what purpose did you do such things?"

Andrew opened his mouth and then closed it again. He could not tell her the truth, of course, for to state outright that it had not been his desire, but rather had come about because of a bet, would make matters all the worse.

"I – I spoke hastily, Lady Carsington," he said, dropping his voice low in the hope that Lord Arthington would not hear him. "I am with my companion and –"

"And he does not wish to admit that he finds himself in a circumstance which he has never been in before," Lord Arthington interrupted, cheerfully. "What Lord Wileham was *attempting* to tell me was that he had no interest in you, Lady Carsington, whereas the opposite, I think, is quite true. The reason he spoke with such vehemence was simply to try to hide that from me, that is all. Pray, do not take offence. I think that would injure Lord Wileham severely, though he would not willingly tell you such a thing either."

Without a chuckle, Lord Arthington slapped him on the shoulder and then turned to walk away, leaving Andrew with a face which burned with fire and eyes which did not know where to look. When they finally fixed themselves on Lady Carsington, she had gone very white indeed, her blue eyes now almost grey as she gazed at him. One hand lifted, her fingers at her mouth and she gave a small, almost imperceptible shake of her head as though she could not quite believe what Lord Arthington had said.

Andrew did not know what to make of this reaction. Was it that she was embarrassed? Or was she horrified to hear that he might have an interest in her?

"You must forgive Lord Arthington." Clearing his throat, Andrew threw out one hand and rolled his eyes, trying to ignore the clawing nervousness which climbed up his throat. "He enjoys trying to mortify me whatever the occasion. He did ask me some very pointed questions and, given that I was concerned about what he would say – and who he might say it to thereafter – I did my best to break up any thought in his mind of a connection between us."

Lady Carsington's hand dropped back to her side, though questions remained in her eyes.

"So you see, I was doing my best to push away his questions," he prevaricated. "I did not mean to insult you. I did not even see that you were nearby, and I apologize for any injury caused."

With a small nod, Lady Carsington looked away from him, her lip catching between her teeth for a brief moment before releasing again. She took a breath and lifted her chin a little, her shoulders straightening, before she finally returned her gaze to his.

"Very well. I shall accept your answer, Lord Wileham, though I confess that I do not know if I am wise to do so, given your reputation."

A wave of relief filled him, and he managed to put on a wry smile.

"I quite understand that, Lady Carsington. Would it help if I was to ask to dance with you this evening? Perhaps that would do more to convince you."

A hint of a smile danced across her lips, though her gaze dropped away.

"You need not do such a thing, Lord Wileham. If you would prefer –"

"I should very much like to dance with you," he stated firmly, surprised that his desire to do so was a genuine one. "Is your dance card full, however?"

She laughed and held out her dance card to him.

"I am an older, widowed lady, Lord Wileham. There are not hordes of gentlemen all wishing to stand up with me, I am afraid!"

"Then they are the foolish ones," he declared, writing his name down for not one but two dances, only pausing when he realized what he had done. His eyes fixed themselves on the second of the dances, his heart beginning to quicken as he tried to steady himself. Never once had he stepped out with a lady for a second time, never before had he permitted himself to do so. Yet, for whatever reason, when it came to Lady Carsington, it seemed that his fervor had him doing things quite outside his own expectations.

This is precisely the opposite of what I said to Lord Arthington.

"Are you quite well?"

Andrew nodded quickly, dragging his eyes away from the dance card and instead, focusing on Lady Carsington's face. Her lip was caught between her teeth again and her blue eyes searched his face. She was clearly aware of how strangely he had been looking at her.

"Yes, quite well." With a forced smile, he handed her the dance card and then clasped his hands behind his back. "We have two dances, Lady Carsington. I hope that will satisfy you?"

"Two?" The way her eyes flared and dropped immediately to the dance card sent a swirling, scurrying sensation into the pit of his stomach but thereafter, when she smiled, it disappeared from him almost immediately. "That is very kind of you, Lord Wileham. I look forward to them both."

"As do I," Andrew answered and, as he stepped away from her, he realized that he meant every word.

～

It was most unlike Andrew to have any sort of nervousness when he stepped out to dance, but on this occasion, with

Lady Carsington, he found himself so filled with anxiety that his breathing was growing quicker with every moment. A single touch of her hand to his was enough to have sweat break out across his forehead.

And then he stumbled.

Heat poured into his face as he corrected himself, barely able to look at Lady Carsington. She took his hand again, and he swallowed at the tightness in his throat and looked straight ahead, the heat which filled him growing all the more as her fingers tightened around his.

Aware that he had not, as yet, said a single word to her since the dance had started, Andrew coughed lightly and then threw her a quick glance, only to note that she was looking at him with great intensity. That single look had the words dying on his lips, stacking up in his throat, and he could not think of how to begin.

"A – a kissing bough, Lord Wileham." Lady Carsington's voice wavered. "It seems as though every couple is stopping beneath it."

The tightness in his throat grew steadily and Andrew could only murmur something indistinct, his heart slamming hard against his ribs as he took in the bough. There were many mistletoe berries on it still, so they could not escape from it by declaring that it was empty. Lady Carsington was quite correct, every couple *was* stopping beneath it, which meant that, if they did not, that would be noted far more than if they simply did as everyone else was.

All the same, the thought of pressing a kiss to Lady Carsington's lips was something Andrew could not seem to contemplate, for his steps wobbled and he turned a little too slowly, embarrassing himself all the more. Lady Carsington clutched at his hand, and he took a breath, steadying himself and, in turn, steadying his resolve.

This was to be a moment like any other, for there had been other Christmas seasons when he had stolen a kiss from under the mistletoe's bough. It had never led to anything further, had never encouraged him to form an attachment with any young lady, and would certainly not do so now.

Except no young lady had ever seemed to draw him in the way that Lady Carsington did.

They were below it now. As if he were in a dream, Andrew reached up and plucked one white berry, holding it between them. Lady Carsington's eyes were upon it also, her lips parting gently as if she might say something to him.

They were not dancing now. Their steps had brought them to a standstill, their gazes now fixed on each other. Short, sharp breaths caught at him, and he lowered his head, praying that he could appear to be as indifferent to her as he had always been with every other lady.

But the touch of her lips against his was like nothing he had ever experienced before. It was only the briefest of moments, a featherlight touch, and yet it was as though fireworks had been set off in the ballroom and were exploding all around him. He could not breathe, he could not think and, even when Lady Carsington said something to him, he could see her lips moving but could not hear a single word she'd said.

When she curtsied, it took him a few seconds to realize what had happened. The music had ended. The dance was over and now all that was required was for him to bow and then step away, leading Lady Carsington back to the side of the ballroom before taking his leave to find the next young lady to dance with.

Dropping into his bow, he lifted his head somewhat stiffly, his arm jutting out towards her so that they might walk together. When she took his arm, he jumped visibly, but did not turn to look at her. Instead, he walked towards the side of the ballroom, saying nothing to her, and hearing blood roaring in his ears.

With one single touch, Lady Carsington had taken apart everything he had ever believed about himself. He was not as unaffected as he had thought. He was not able to step away from the lady and simply forget about her. Instead, the imprint of her lips on his remained, as though it had burned itself into his skin, so that he could not forget it.

"Thank you, Lord Wileham."

Lady Carsington's eyes were searching his face, but Andrew could only glance at her and then turn his head away. With a brief nod, he turned on his heel and stalked away from her, wishing that he had never thought to ask her to dance in the first place.

CHAPTER TEN

That kiss meant something to him.
"You are not paying me the least bit of attention, Julianna."

Julianna blinked and attempted to focus on Lady Gilford.

"My apologies. My thoughts were elsewhere."

Her friend smiled.

"I quite understand. You were thinking of *someone* else?"

Hesitating, Julianna wondered whether she ought to share with her friend what had taken place. Lady Gilford would not judge her, of course, but she might be somewhat surprised to hear what had gone on.

But then again, what exactly *had* taken place? It had not been anything of real importance, for while she had danced with Lord Wileham, and they had shared a brief kiss under the mistletoe bough, it was not as though they had been the only couple to do such a thing. Everyone who had danced and then stopped under the bough had done so, which meant that there had been nothing of significance in the particular moment which she had shared with Lord Wileham.

"Goodness, it must be something of grave importance to have you thinking so deeply!"

Lady Gilford set her tea to one side and looked straight at Julianna, shook her head and inwardly battled over what it was she would say by way of explanation.

"I – I overheard Lord Wileham speaking about me to Lord Arthington," she said, beginning at the start of what had taken place. "He said to him that he had no intention whatsoever of furthering his acquaintance with me."

"While, at the same time, hoping to garner your attentions towards him," Lady Gilford stated, dryly. "Goodness, he is a gentleman who never changes! I saw him dance with you last evening *and* steal a kiss by going to stand under the mistletoe bough."

A flash of heat ran straight through Julianna.

"Yes, he did."

"How embarrassing that must have been for you." Lady Gilford tutted and shook her head. "That gentleman is one of the worst of fellows I think I have ever seen in London. It is not that he is a rake – for that would make it obvious to all who knew him – but he is worse than that. He does not have liaisons, he does not toy with any young lady in the hope of a physical connection but, rather, he seeks to linger in their thoughts and in their minds. He wants every young lady in London to think of him, to respond to *him,* so that he might have all of their attention. How much he loves to be admired and revered! His pride is so great, it must continually be fed, and he attempts to do so, even with you! That, I think, is the most disingenuous thing about him; the fact that he garners attention simply for *himself* rather than because he feels any real interest in the ladies whom he surrounds himself with."

Julianna's response caught in her throat, shame beginning to burn a path up her spine and into her heart. Whatever was she doing? It was foolish for her to have any feelings for Lord Wileham. She knew that, but for whatever reason, her heart was continually insisting that it turn itself towards him. Lady Gilford was right, she should *not* be thinking of him with any hope of having her feelings returned. He was doing what he could to pull her into his sphere but, as her friend had said, he had no intention of pursing things further with her. Why was she so foolish? Why had she let herself become so caught up with him? After what she had overheard between Lord Wileham and Lord Arthington, could she really trust his explanation? Or had he said all of those things in an attempt to garner her trust again, so that he might pull her attention towards himself again?

"You have gone a little pale, Julianna."

Lady Gilford's eyebrows lifted, but before she could ask a question, Julianna smiled and rose to her feet.

"I am quite well. I was thinking that I should like to go into town this afternoon."

"Into town?" Lady Gilford repeated, though her smile quickly followed. "A capital idea! It is not snowing today, and it will still be daylight for at least another hour or so. Where should you like to go?"

"Anywhere," Julianna stated, thinking that the best thing for her to do, to remove Lord Wileham from her thoughts, was to distract herself somehow. "The bookshop, mayhap?"

Lady Gilford made a face.

"And here I was hoping for a few new ribbons or a pair

of gloves," she laughed, as Julianna smiled and went to ring the bell, so they might have the carriage prepared. "I am certain that there will be enough time to go to both, however."

"I think so." With a smile, Julianna returned to her friend. "Thank you for indulging me."

"But of course. A walk through town – though it will be cold – is precisely what we both need."

∼

"Lord Pleasanton."

Julianna's spirits immediately crashed to the floor as the gentleman inclined his head towards her. They had not spoken since their disastrous walk in the park together, the one where Lord Wileham had interrupted them, and Julianna could not imagine what sort of reception she would have from him. Having walked into the bookshop to be faced with that gentleman, Julianna had not been given any other choice but to greet him, though she had no desire to.

"Lady Carsington." Lord Pleasanton lifted his head. "And Lady Gilford, good afternoon."

"Good afternoon."

She made to move past him, but Lord Pleasanton put out one hand to stop her, though he dropped it quickly back to his side thereafter.

"I wonder if I might have a moment to apologize, Lady Carsington," he said, his voice low and quiet – perhaps to ensure that Lady Gilford did not overhear him, but also since they were in a quiet shop. "I am aware that I behaved badly, and I want now to apologize for my mistake."

Julianna did not know what to think. Lord Pleasanton

had already surprised her once before, by how he had behaved. Was there a chance that he might do so again?

"Pray excuse me."

Lady Gilford stepped away, but not before she had shot Julianna a look which Julianna herself took to be a warning. Having already explained to her friend what had taken place previously, Lady Gilford was clearly a little concerned over what the outcome of this meeting would be, a concern Julianna shared.

"A *few* moments," she emphasized.

Lord Pleasanton nodded fervently and then, much to Julianna's dislike, took her by the elbow and led her across the bookshop so that they might stand and talk without being overheard. Quickly, she removed her elbow from his grip as soon as she could, aware of the crawling sensation which climbed up her skin as he looked at her.

"My most profound apologies for what took place between us, Lady Carsington."

"Took place *between* us?" she repeated, before he could say anything more. "Lord Pleasanton, if I recall correctly, I did nothing other than step out with you for a short walk through the park. It was *you* who decided to behave unpleasantly."

Lord Pleasanton frowned.

"I only wished to make my intentions clear. I think –"

"Rather than expressing yourself carefully and with great consideration, you chose to fling questions at me – some most inappropriate and intimate, I might add," she continued, interrupting him before he could continue absolving himself in his own eyes. "You did not leave me to explain my thoughts as regarded my future in my own time, but rather threw question after question at me about my late husband and my considerations with respect to marrying again! I could not quite believe my ears – and then, when I told you that I found your questions somewhat improper and much too forward, you took that very badly indeed, and expressed yourself in a... somewhat ungentlemanly way, do you not think?"

This was his opportunity to agree with her, to state that yes, he *had* behaved poorly, and Julianna waited for him to take it, wanting him to see that what she said had merit and that her own considerations were of importance. Lord Pleasanton puffed his chest out, standing as tall as he could, his eyes fixed to hers with an impervious gaze and slowly, Julianna's hopes began to sink. It was not that she wanted Lord Pleasanton to consider her for matrimony, but more that she merely wanted the respect due to her, as well as his apology.

"I was, mayhap, a little ungallant in my manner." The sniff told her that he was not entirely in agreement with what she had said of him. "For that, I do apologize. I should not have put my questions to you in such a thoughtless manner. Even though you have been widowed for three years, it is understandable that you should still have some feelings for your late husband."

Julianna's lip curled. She did not much like Lord Pleasanton's manner. He had told her that he wished to apologize only to then deliver what was, to her mind, one of the worst apologies she had ever received. It was, she felt, an attempt to place most of the blame onto her, and her lingering emotions about her status as widow – which she certainly was *not* going to accept.

"Lord Pleasanton, I –"

The door opened and, before she could say anything more, her eyes caught sight of Lord Wileham who had also come into the bookshop. He shook the snow from his hat and Julianna quickly realized, with a glance out of the window, that there was considerable snow falling again.

"You were saying, Lady Carsington?"

Lord Pleasanton's prompting forced Julianna to regain herself, and she dragged her gaze away from Lord Wileham, her heart thumping painfully.

"Yes. Lord Pleasanton, what I was saying was –"

"Have you come to shelter from the snow also?" Lord Wileham came towards them, a gentle smile on his face – though that quickly faded when he glanced at Lord Pleasanton. "Good afternoon, Lord Pleasanton. I had not thought..." Trailing off, he cleared his throat and shrugged lightly. "It does not matter what I thought. The snow has become rather heavy, has it not?"

"It was not snowing when I came inside," Julianna replied, suddenly not quite certain where to look, and feeling the tension wind tight strings around her heart. "This was merely an accidental meeting." It felt as if she were making an excuse to Lord Wileham for why she was in company with another gentleman and, with a lift of her chin, she gestured to Lord Pleasanton. "Though we were in the midst of a somewhat important conversation."

"Oh." Lord Wileham glanced towards Julianna and then looked away again. "Forgive me for the interruption."

Much to Julianna's surprise, Lord Wileham did not move away – and this, despite his apology! She could not understand why he was so eager to remain, only to then recall what Lady Gilford had said. Lord Wileham sought only to garner as much attention for himself as he could and *she* was the one he was, at present, focusing his interest on. He wanted her to think only of him, to be so distracted by his presence that she would stammer and stumble through her conversation with Lord Pleasanton – and to her great shame, Julianna realized that what Lord Wileham wanted, she was giving him. The truth was, she *was* distracted by his presence, found her thoughts going entirely towards him instead of lingering on her conversation with Lord Pleasanton. All he had to do was give her a single look and she found herself tongue-tied, lost in thought over what it was he wanted to say to her and what, in return, she would then say to him.

I must stop this, she told herself, firmly. *I must remove my interest in Lord Wileham from my heart without hesitation, else I shall be the one to make a fool of myself.*

"I believe you were about to ask me to take another walk with you, Lord Pleasanton, in order to make up for our previous attempt," she said, swiftly, as Lord Pleasanton's eyebrows lifted. "And I, I think, was about to accept."

"Is that so?" Lord Wileham looked from Julianna to Lord Pleasanton and back again. "I do hope I shall not have to break apart your second walk and carry Lady Carsington away from you, as I did the first time!"

While Lord Wileham laughed, Julianna and Lord Pleasanton did not. Instead, they looked at one another and then each turned their gaze in another direction. Lord Pleasanton's face had gone a little white and Julianna was sure that her face was red, given just how hot it felt at present. It was embarrassing to be reminded of what had taken place – though she did not feel as though she had any culpability herself – but it came from a place of embarrassment over Lord Wileham' brash manner in speaking.

"Our walk then, Lady Carsington?" Lord Pleasanton turned to her, clearly deciding that it would be best to continue with their conversation rather than engage with Lord Wileham. "Yes, I think another walk together would be good, for it would help us both to put aside our past difficulties, would it not?"

"I think it would."

Quite where the idea had come from, Julianna could not say but something about seeing Lord Wileham and realizing how she felt about him – as well as recalling what Lady Gilford had said – made her quite determined that she would *not* permit herself to be pulled into his sphere. Thus, the suggestion of another walk with Lord Pleasanton had come out of her mouth, even though that was something she certainly did not wish to do. Now, however, she could not refuse him and thus, she was forced to smile back at him as though she were pleased this had taken place.

"Shall we say in two days hence? And if the weather is as atrocious as it is at present, then I should be glad to call upon you, if that is not too forward?"

The glint in his eye as he spoke the latter part of his sentence made Julianna's smile drop. Was he attempting to tease her? To state, in his way, that he did not think that what she had said about his past behavior had any relevance? Surely it could not be so!

"Lady Carsington?"

Her eyes closed and she took a breath.

"Two days hence, Lord Pleasanton."

With a nod, she made to excuse herself, only for her eyes to catch on Lord Wileham. He was gazing at her with the most curious expression, and one that she could not quite make out, for it was as if he had never truly seen her before. There was an intensity, a sharpness in his eyes which had her burning from the inside out, a softness about his mouth that immediately brought to mind the kiss they had shared – and being reminded of that had her turning away from them both.

As she walked, Julianna kept her head lifted and her back straight, but the pain in her chest only grew. This afternoon had been quite disastrous. Instead of finding herself a little happier, a little less inclined to think of Lord Wileham, she was now all of a muddle. She was walking away from the one gentleman who was attempting to push his way into her heart and entering into the furthering of an acquaintance with a gentleman she did not care for in the least! Embarrassed and confused, Julianna passed one hand over her eyes and tried not to lose herself in frustration. She had to maintain her composure – outwardly, at least – until Lord Pleasanton and Lord Wileham were no longer in her view.

And then, mayhap, it was time for her to tell Lady Gilford everything, embarrassing though it might be. If she was to have any enjoyment this Christmas, then this was no longer a burden she could carry alone.

CHAPTER ELEVEN

*A*ndrew scowled and slammed his coins down on the table, making his bet.

"You do not appear to be in the best of spirits." Lord Dorchester lifted an eyebrow. "Is there any particular reason?"

Glowering at him, Andrew stayed silent and waited as the turn passed to the next person. Lord Dorchester was the cause of all of this, he reasoned, so thus, he had no right to ask him anything about his present circumstances.

"It cannot be that you are bored and dulled by having to only focus your attentions upon one lady in particular?" Lord Whitaker remarked, picking up a glass of whisky. "Come now, I thought you would find that a rather intriguing task!"

"It is certainly nothing of the sort." Ignoring the pain in his chest as he recalled Lady Carsington and Lord Pleasanton standing together, he shrugged and sniffed. "How long am I to go on with attempting to show an interest in Lady Carsington?"

Lord Rushford glanced around the table, then shrugged.

"I suppose until Christmas Day? We had not specified, but I think that Christmas Day is more than enough of a punishment."

Andrew groaned aloud.

"That is still over a fortnight from now!"

"Do not tell me you are to give up?" Lord Rushford chuckled. "If you do not fulfill the consequences placed upon you, then we shall have to think of something more, come the spring Season."

Hating the smile on Lord Rushford's face, Andrew scowled darkly.

"I *shall* endure, but it is rather difficult when I have no interest in the lady and yet I am forced to continue attempting to speak with her and dance with her. It is all incredibly mediocre, given that she has no desire to continue in her acquaintance with me!"

"Well, that is absolutely false!" Lord Arthington laughed, rolling his eyes as the other gentlemen looked at him, though Andrew's jaw set tight. "I saw her reaction to you when she overheard you speaking with me. That was a lady who was offended!"

"As she had every right to be," Andrew said, quickly, eager that the other gentlemen did not take what Lord Arthington had said with any seriousness. "To explain, gentlemen, I spoke harshly about my present circumstances and Lady Carsington was standing only a little behind me – though I did not know it at the time. She was quite insulted, though you need not worry, Rushford, I did not tell her of the bet and the consequences which have been dealt to me thereafter."

Seeing the other gentlemen chuckle, he shot a look at Lord Arthington, but his friend did not seem to notice, and something like despair settled into Andrew's heart. Why was it that Lord Arthington was so utterly unreliable? He spoke without thinking, without even *considering,* and that was beginning to irritate Andrew a good deal.

He blinked, then frowned. He had not always found Lord Arthington to be so. It had only been recently and, on both occasions, had come at the time when he spoke of Lady Carsington. Surely it could not be that the lady was having such a profound effect on him that he was now even seeing his friends in an entirely different light?

This cannot be.

"It is you, Wileham."

With a grunt, Andrew threw his cards on the table and rose from his chair.

"I am finished."

Leaving all of the money he had bet in the center of the table, he walked out of the card room and made his way directly to the door of the gambling den. The air was cold and crisp, and he closed his eyes, never once stopping as he walked out into the street. Ignoring his carriage, he strode down the street, heedless as to where he was going, one hand rubbing over his eyes. Having left his hat, gloves, and coat back at the gambling den, it did not take long for his entire body to begin to flood with cold, but Andrew welcomed it, grateful for the sharpness it brought to his thoughts.

Why was it that Lady Carsington had such a hold on him? Surely it could not be the lady herself?

The dim light above him gave him entry to St James' Park and, even though it was dark, and his breath frosted the air, Andrew stepped into it and continued to walk, his hands balling into fists as he went.

"It is because I have been unable to behave as I might

otherwise wish to," he told himself, aloud. "That is all. There is no other reason for it. It is not that Lady Carsington... Julianna..."

With a groan, he stopped dead and scrubbed at his eyes with both fists as though doing so would remove the image of her from his memory. It did not do so, of course, for there she lingered and, as Andrew dropped his hands, a heaviness came into his shoulders, making him slump a little.

It had been that kiss, that moment when he had pressed his lips to hers. It had been barely even a moment, a breath passed between them, and yet he could still feel the sparks it had created whispering through him whenever he brought it to mind. To know that, now, he would have to linger in his attentions on her until Christmas Day was come and gone was a torture which he did not think he could face. It was causing him so much difficulty, so much inner pain, that it was too great a burden to bear.

"Perhaps I should return home."

It was an almost unthinkable thing to do, for returning to his estate for Christmas Day was not something he had done in many a year. Prior to taking on the title, he had spent the day with family and, thereafter, with his friends either at their respective estates or here in London. To go back to his own manor house, and to stay there, quite alone, and with such torturous thoughts as these, was almost more than he could bear to even imagine.

And yet, what was the alternative? To stay here in London, aware that he was struggling with his attraction to Lady Carsington, and wishing that he could do something to remove her from his heart? Considering the two options, Andrew could not quite decide which would be the worse.

With a roar of frustration, he threw his head back and his arms wide as though the ink dark skies would somehow reveal the answer to him, but there came nothing beyond the cold wind whipping about him, and heavy darkness drawing towards him.

Andrew closed his eyes and let out another frustrated breath, beginning to shiver now. The nip of the winter wind had begun to make its way to his skin, finding the gaps between his shirt buttons and the collar at his neck. With feet like lead, Andrew made his way back towards the entrance of the park and began to wander in the direction of the gambling den. His thoughts grew murky, his head hanging low as he shivered violently, a little surprised that he did not seem to care about how cold he was. His feet took him in whichever direction they wished and, as he walked, the snow began to fall heavily.

His steps grew sluggish and, lifting his head, Andrew attempted to make out where he was. There were no lights anywhere, and the dim glow from the lanterns offered nothing more than a gray shadow. He was shaking so violently, his whole body was shuddering, his bones rattling and his teeth chattering. A wave of panic pushed a little more energy into his limbs, and he walked faster now, hands rubbing at his arms, breathing heavily as he fought to find shelter. Anywhere would do, any place he might seek to step into to be free from the wind and the snow – but nothing presented itself. Out of desperation, he began to knock on every door he came to, but they remained shut tight and windows barred.

Desperation began to claw at his throat and, as he looked around into the gloom, fear lodged itself directly into his heart and mind. If he did not find safety, if he did not find shelter, then the danger of death was very real – and approaching him with ever increasing haste as the doors remained locked to him.

Andrew shivered again and closed his eyes, trying to think clearly, but finding nothing but mist there instead. He did not know what to do. He did not know where he was or where to go.

He was lost.

CHAPTER TWELVE

*J*ulianna leaned her head back against the squabs and let out a slow, contented breath. That evening had been *very* pleasant indeed and, much to her relief, Lord Wileham had not been present, which had given her clarity of mind for the first time in many days. As yet, she had not spoken to either of her friends about her conflicting feelings for the gentleman and, given that he had not been in attendance, she had not felt the need to do so.

Turning her head to look out of the window, Julianna narrowed her eyes in an attempt to make out the scene. While she had been at dinner with her friends and acquaintances, a heavy snowfall had added to the snow already lying on the ground, and the roads – which had been a good deal easier to make out on her arrival – had been almost impossible to see when the carriage had departed, though the coachman had assured her that he would be able to get her back to the townhouse quite safely, albeit much more slowly than she was used to. Julianna did not mind in the least, for even though she was already cold, it was preferable to remain safe rather than insist that the coachman rush home.

A sudden movement caught her attention. The street lanterns offered very little by way of light, but all the same, she saw a shadow moving. Her hands flew to her mouth, and she caught her breath, suddenly afraid that they were about to be set upon by a group of ruffians, only for the shadow to let out a cry for help. Staggering forward, the person then practically threw themselves towards the carriage and, with a shriek, Julianna lurched away from the window. The coachman came to an immediate stop and Julianna closed her eyes tight, her stomach roiling. Had they accidentally hit whoever it was, who had come out of the shadows? She did not know what would happen, if they had done so.

"What do you think you're doing?" The rough, rasping voice of the driver had Julianna's eyes shut, her throat closing up as fear lodged itself tight in her chest. There came no response from the person on the street and as she waited, Julianna heard the driver climbing down from his seat.

"You there, get up! Get yourself away from my Lady's carriage."

A groan emanated from the darkness and Julianna dropped her hands to her lap, her head rolling back as she let out a slow breath of relief. Whoever it was had not been killed, then.

"Be off with you! I – oh."

Julianna sat up straight, her eyes widening as there came a rap on the door. Opening it, she saw the coachman's wide eyes looking back at her, the carriage lanterns illuminating his features.

"My Lady. This fellow is in a bad way," he said, slowly,

turning a little to gesture to whoever it was. "I think – I think he's just fainted. What should I do?"

The knot in her throat began to loosen as she looked down at the ground behind the coachman but saw nothing other than snow and shadows.

"He has fainted?"

"Yes."

"And we cannot leave him for he will surely freeze to death," she finished, as the coachman nodded. "You are a good man, Mr. Grant, to be so considerate."

The coachman ducked his head.

"Thank you, my Lady. I should not like to be responsible for the death of anyone, and I believe that the good Lord has told us we must always care for the less fortunate."

"That He has," Julianna agreed, her hands clasping together tightly as she took a deep breath. It was clear to her what she had to do, but there was a good deal of fear lingering still. "Then you must place the fellow here, in the carriage with me. Quickly now." Resolved, she shifted and gestured to the seat opposite. "I have a blanket here that he can have. No doubt he is already freezing."

The coachman nodded and stepped away for a few moments, though Julianna heard him huffing and puffing with the obvious strain of lifting the fellow towards the carriage. The coachman reached the door, half dragging the unconscious man, and she did her best to aid him as they, somehow, managed to get the prone figure into the carriage. Covering him with a blanket, Julianna shivered lightly, looking back at the coachman.

"I will knock if there is something wrong," she said, hearing the slight tremor in her voice. "Go. Quickly. We must get him back to the house."

Swallowing her fear, she took a steadying breath and

reached forward to put the blanket over the man a little more – only for recognition to flare.

"Wileham?" Her hand flew to her mouth, her eyes wide as she stared into his face. The carriage shifted as the horses moved forward, and the carriage-light swung gently, shifting light across his face. With a thundering heart, she grasped his hand, feeling the cold in his fingers and sensing fear rising in her heart. She could not imagine why he had been out in the middle of London without any companions, nor why he wore no coat, hat or gloves but, given his pallor and the chill of his hand when she grasped it, he had been out of doors for some time.

"Oh, Wileham!"

Fright had her taking the blankets from her own lap and placing them upon him, realizing now just how wet his clothes were from the snow. When she brushed back his hair from his forehead, her fingers came away damp, and tears began to burn in Julianna's eyes. She did not know what he had been doing or what would become of him, but there was a very real danger now that he could become very ill indeed.

Closing her eyes, Julianna murmured a prayer and clasped one of Lord Wileham's hands in both of her own. The sooner they could get him into the townhouse and warm again, the more relieved she would be – but with the snow still falling and the carriage making slow progress through the London streets, just how long would it be?

∽

"He is in bed now, my Lady."

Julianna turned her head to look at the maid who had stepped into the parlor.

"Awake?"

"I couldn't say, my Lady."

"And the Physician?"

"He has been sent for, but the messenger has not returned as yet, my Lady." The maid bit her lip then dropped her head. "It is so very cold and there is so much snow that..." Trailing off, she said nothing more, but Julianna understood exactly what it was that she meant. If the messenger had not yet returned, then the chances of the Physician making it to the townhouse with any speed were few and far between.

Which meant that it would be up to her to look after Lord Wileham.

"Very well." Taking a deep breath, she set her shoulders and marched towards the door. "Then I will go to him at once." Her face heated as she paused, looking at the maid. "His clothes?"

"Are being washed at present, my Lady. The butler has seen that Lord Wileham is dressed in something clean and dry."

"And he is presentable?"

"Yes, my Lady."

With a nod, Julianna made her way out of the parlor without another word, finding herself almost breaking into a run as she mounted the stairs to the bedrooms above. There had been no question of Lord Wileham being brought here – she would not have stood for anything else. She could not have had the coachman take him back to his own townhouse, for the snow was much too strong and she had no assurance that he would be able to take him home and thereafter, return her to the townhouse safely. Thankfully, her servants had worked quickly, and without even a word of surprise over the situation, with both the butler and the housekeeper making certain that everything went smoothly. Julianna had retired to the parlor until he had been changed and was able to rest, but she had done nothing but pace up and down the room, waiting for news of his condition.

Pausing outside the door, Julianna closed her eyes, drew in strength, and then stepped inside. There was only one maid present, setting out a blanket by the fire so it might warm a little before she placed it on the bed. Julianna nodded to her, but then returned her attention to Lord Wileham, her heart in her throat as she drew closer to the bed.

Lord Wileham was white-faced, his eyes were closed and there were deep shadows beneath them. His chest rose and fell but, aside from that, there was no sign of life. Tears began to burn again in Julianna's eyes, but she steeled herself with an effort, refusing to let them fall. Tears and upset would not help Lord Wileham and, even though at this moment she felt both helpless and distraught, such emotions would have to be set to the side if she was to help him.

"The tea-tray?"

The maid turned at once and brought it over, from where it had been sitting on a small table near the fire, before setting it down next to Julianna.

"The butler also said a little brandy would help, my Lady." Gesturing to the glass on the tray, she stepped back as Julianna picked it up, glancing doubtfully at Lord Wileham. "If I might, my Lady, my brother was ill like this one time when I was younger. My father got a spoon and put a little brandy onto my brother's lips, because he wasn't awake enough to drink it."

Julianna nodded, not trusting her voice. Reaching for the spoon, she smiled as best she could at the maid who, nodding, smiled briefly and then stepped away again. With the spoon in one hand and the glass of brandy in the other, Julianna looked at Lord Wileham. Her heart ached furiously, and she blinked rapidly to keep the tears at bay. With a shaking hand, she took a small measure of brandy in the teaspoon, and then brought it to Lord Wileham's lips.

It was only enough to dampen them, a tiny trickle darting into the corner of his mouth – but Lord Wileham did not so much as flinch. There was no movement at all, save for his breathing, and Julianna pressed her lips together tight, heat still behind her eyes.

You must waken, Lord Wileham, she prayed silently. *I have no one else to help you.*

Again, she took the tiniest amount of brandy she could and brushed it lightly across his lips. Afraid he might choke if she put too much into his mouth, she set it aside and then, reaching for his hand, held it tightly and bowed her head. The only thing she could do now was pray. Lord Wileham was dry, he was warm, but he was still unconscious, and she did not know what else could be done for him.

How long she prayed for, she did not know. The sound of the fire crackling in the grate and the howl of the wind at the window had her both comforted and trembling in equal measure, knowing the power the latter had to steal life. The maid came and put another heated blanket over Lord Wileham, and then went to fetch Julianna a fresh tea tray, seeing that the first had become cold – and still, Julianna prayed.

Her heart was pounding, her stomach twisting with worry about what would happen to Lord Wileham if he did not waken, or if she could not get the Physician to him. With the weather as bad as it was, it seemed unlikely that they should have any help tonight, and perhaps not even tomorrow – and by then, would it be too late?

A single tear dropped from her eyes and fell onto Lord Wileham's fingers as she clasped them in her own. Julianna squeezed them tightly closed again, only to hear a small, barely audible sound.

Her head lifted, her gaze turning to Lord Wileham's face. Though his eyes were still closed, he had swallowed and now his tongue was touching the edges of his lips.

A fresh hope filled her, and Julianna dropped her head and sobbed out of sheer relief.

Lord Wileham was awake.

CHAPTER THIRTEEN

*S*omething sharp was on his lips. Andrew could not work out what it was – in truth, he could not understand very much at all. It felt as though he had been trying to awaken from a deep and fearful dream, but his consciousness would not let him escape from it.

"Here."

A voice that seemed to come from very far away reached him and Andrew frowned, trying to open his eyes, but lacking any sort of strength by which to do so. A gentle hand touched his head, lifting him a little as a glass settled against his lips. It took him all the energy he had, just to take two small sips - though his body craved a good deal more. The hand released him, and he rested back on the soft pillows, realizing slowly that he was in a bed.

It took him some time before he had the strength to try to open his eyes again. With a groan, he managed to crack one eye open, and the scene slowly came into view. The other opened with an effort and, all the more confused, Andrew looked into the face of none other than Lady Carsington.

For a moment, a terror gripped him, but it soon faded when he took in the situation a little better, his consciousness returning to him more fully. Lady Carsington was not in bed with him, but was beside him, still fully clothed, though her hands were gripping one of his. Her face was rather white, her eyes rounded, and she looked as though she had been crying.

Slowly, Andrew let his gaze run over the rest of the room, taking in the unfamiliarity of his circumstances. He was not in his own bed, nor in his own room. Which meant that, given Lady Carsington's presence, he was in her townhouse. What cause had he to be here?

"Take a little more brandy." Letting go of his hand, Lady Carsington rose and took the brandy glass from the tray before bringing it to his lips again. Andrew took another sip and let the liquor bring a little more warmth and strength to his limbs, though his throat ached terribly when he tried to speak.

"Why am I here?"

Lady Carsington looked back at him steadily, taking his hand again.

"You do not remember?"

Andrew closed his eyes.

"No."

"My coachman was taking me back home when a figure stepped out of the thickly falling snow – almost falling into the path of my carriage. My coachman stopped to make certain that you were quite all right – and to berate you as well – but then you fainted."

"You brought me here?" The rasping in his voice pained him with every word he spoke, but he forced them out regardless. "To your home?"

Lady Carsington nodded.

"The weather is dreadful. The snow is falling in sheets and, thus, the only thing I could do was have you brought back to my townhouse. In truth, I did not know it was you until the coachman had placed you in the carriage."

Closing his eyes, Andrew took a ragged breath, suddenly recalling what had happened. Pain shot through his head, and he winced, hearing Lady Carsington's murmur of concern.

"I became lost," he whispered, hoping that would help the pain in his throat. "I was with friends at a gambling den, and stepped outside for a moment."

He did not say a word to her about his reason for stepping away from his friends in such a manner, nor about the fact that he had lost himself in despondency and confusion over his desire to become closer to her, finding himself a little ashamed of his own reckless behavior. He had endangered his own life by his foolishness. She did not need to know about that.

"I thank God it was my carriage you fell near," Lady Carsington answered, as the door opened behind her. "I do not know what would have become of you otherwise."

"I should return home." Andrew opened his eyes again to see the maid setting out a fresh tray of tea and the like on the table. "I shall remove myself and –"

"That is not necessary." Lady Carsington gripped his hand with a little more strength. "You cannot even lift your head, Lord Wileham, so I certainly do not think that you will be able to even rise from the bed, let alone make your way through the snow!" A glimmer came into her eyes and Andrew frowned at it, wondering if she was angry with him, only to see tears clinging to her lashes. Shame burned through him, and he closed his eyes again to shut out the sight. He did not deserve any of Lady Carsington's kindness towards him, did not deserve her tears. The only reason he had been pursuing her company was because he had lost a bet which had then led to him walking about in the snow as he fought to make sense of all that he felt. This was his own doing, and yet she was the one bearing the brunt of his suffering. She had taken great pains to take care of him, being gentle and tender in her consideration, and yet the only reason he was here in the first place was because of his own foolishness. "Besides which," Lady Carsington continued, as Andrew kept his eyes closed, "the weather has decided to remain as dreadful as it was when I first found you. I do not think that you would be able to return home, even if you wished to."

Andrew cleared his throat as best he could, wincing with the stabbing pain which shot through his chest.

"I do not deserve this consideration, Lady Carsington."

"Nonsense."

When he opened his eyes, Lady Carsington was pouring tea for them both and, determined that she was not going to lift the cup to his mouth as she had done before, Andrew placed his hands to either side and attempted to push himself up. Lady Carsington immediately rose to help him and, though it pained him to have to accept it, he did so without a word. Soon, he was sitting up and, though he immediately wanted to do nothing more than lie down again and sleep, Andrew accepted the China cup from Lady Carsington and sipped at it. The sweetness of the tea settled into him, and he took a deep breath, feeling a little better than he had before.

Then he coughed and even Lady Carsington winced at the sound.

"I think you shall have to remain abed and warm for some days," she murmured, reaching out to brush hair from his forehead and letting her fingers run lightly down his cheek, her eyes searching his face though her touch, Andrew told himself, came from consideration rather than from anything akin to affection. "Please, do not force yourself from this place before you are ready. I should not like to see you become worse."

He nodded; his chest tight.

"Was I in a very dreadful state when you found me?"

She looked back at him.

"What do you remember?"

"Being very cold," he answered, the bleakness he had felt returning to him like a shroud. "The doors I knocked on were not answered, and I was utterly lost. I feared for my life."

His voice as he spoke these last few words was hoarse, and Lady Carsington immediately grasped his hand tightly again, her eyes meeting his.

"Which is why I beg of you to stay for as long as it takes you to recover, regardless of the weather outside," she said, a hint of pleading in her voice. "When you were placed in the carriage, your skin was white, your clothes soaked with the snow and your hair damp. I cannot express to you the –"

Stopping short, she dropped her head, clearly attempting to regain her composure, and a lump formed in Andrew's throat. This lady had endured a great deal in rescuing him, and he did not think that he could ever find the words to thank her for what she had done.

"I am going to be quite well."

It was the only thing that came to his lips to say and Lady Carsington, with a sniff and a watery smile, lifted her head and looked back at him.

"Yes, you shall be," she said, with more firmness than he had expected. "For you are not going to leave this house until you are just as well as you have always been. Do I make myself quite clear, Lord Wileham?"

He nodded. The sweetness of her, and the kindness in her eyes was almost more than he could bear. For a moment, the desire to tell her everything about the bet, about his change of feelings, and about the battle which had sent him out into the snow, rushed over him and he opened his mouth to say something, only to snap it closed again as Lady Carsington pulled out a handkerchief and dabbed at her eyes.

She had endured enough for one evening. The truth, he decided, would have to wait for another time. After all of this, Andrew felt as though he had no choice but to reveal everything to her.

∼

"THE YULE LOG?"

Lady Carsington nodded, smiling at him as she pushed her embroidery needle through.

"Yes, do you not have one?"

Andrew frowned.

"I do not think that I have ever had a yule log within my own townhouse, though it is a tradition I grew up with, of course."

"I am quite determined to have one, even though I am in London," Lady Carsington declared, though her eyes went to the window. "Though perhaps the weather will prevent me from doing so."

Glancing at the window and seeing the snow still falling heavily outside, Andrew smiled at Lady Carsington as she sighed.

"I am determined that you shall have one, Lady Carsington. Even if the snow is up to my shoulders, I shall go and fetch you one from... wherever one finds such things from."

To his relief, Lady Carsington laughed, and Andrew grinned at her. She then went into great detail about how she and her family had gone out in search of the yule log every year, combing her father's estate for the very best log, which would burn for many days, and how she had enjoyed every moment of the hunt. Andrew enjoyed listening to her, but all the more, loved the smile which settled on her face as she spoke. There was a soft shimmer in her eyes, a reminder of memories long past and, as she continued, Andrew's heart began to turn towards her all the more.

That caused the smile on his face to become rather stiff. That had been the very reason he had left the gambling den in the first place, the cause of his walk through the snow. Having identified the feelings in his heart – which were unsettling, to say the least – he had been attempting to work out what he was meant to do but now, circumstances had led him to be sitting in the house of the very lady he was trying to forget. She had taken great care of him these last two days, aiding in his recovery and insisting that the Physician – who had finally managed to make it to the house some two days after he had been called for – see him without delay, even though Andrew had been feeling much improved. The Physician had remarked upon how much Lady Carsington had done, and had made it quite clear that, had she not behaved as she had done, then Andrew might now be gravely ill indeed.

An uncomfortable twisting settled in his stomach, and he looked away from Lady Carsington towards the roaring fire next to him. He had determined to tell her the truth about the bet, foolish though it was, and the consequences which had been laid on him thereafter, but the words simply would not come to him. In the three days he had been with Lady Carsington, his desire for her closeness, for her companionship, had grown to such a significance that he could not free himself from it, not even if he had wanted to.

"I shall have to return home tomorrow, I think."

When his eyes went to hers, Lady Carsington was no longer smiling.

"I suppose you should," she murmured, her gaze dropping away quickly. "So long as you are recovered enough."

"I am."

"Your throat and your chest no longer pain you?"

He lifted one shoulder, a rueful smile on his lips.

"There is some pain, and my cough comes occasionally, but it is better than before." Taking a breath, he pushed away the desire to remain exactly where he was for another day or so, knowing that the only reason he wanted it was so that he might be in company with Lady Carsington for a little longer. "Given that there has been no more snow this last day, I think that the roads will be safe enough for the carriage to get through, though I have not heard any passing by these last few days. No-one has been out walking either, though I cannot blame them for staying indoors, given how deep the snow has become!"

Lady Carsington nodded, glancing at him again before turning her head towards the fire.

"I am sure that no one in the *ton* will be aware of your presence here, Lord Wileham."

Andrew frowned, shifting in his chair.

"I did not mean to express any sort of worry about that, Lady Carsington," he said, softly. "I do not care about that in the least, though I should want your reputation to be protected."

The edge of her mouth lifted, though her eyes remained settled on the fire.

"Thank you, Lord Wileham. I appreciate your concern."

"And I appreciate your kindness," he said, speaking without even thinking about how best to express what he wanted to say. "We were at odds, I think, were we not? We have found ourselves in a strange world, where we are connected and thrust apart – mostly by my own foolishness – and then find we are thrust together again in the most unexpected manner."

Lady Carsington's eyes glinted as she smiled, looking at him again.

"That is true. Though I am glad that we were pushed together in this way, Lord Wileham, for I dread to think of what would have happened, had you been left walking in the snow." Her smile slipped. "The consequences of that –"

"Are not worth thinking of," he stated, firmly. "As I have said, I am more grateful to you than I can express. I – I am sorry that you missed your walk with Lord Pleasanton."

"I am not."

Lady Carsington's eyes flared, and she clapped one hand to her mouth as Andrew stared at her, his heart leaping about in his chest. And then, he let out a bark of laughter which was swiftly followed by Lady Carsington giggling, her face flushed and her eyes bright. She shook her head and Andrew laughed all the harder, the room filled with the sound of their mirth.

"Good gracious, I should not have said such a thing," she exclaimed, her cheeks now a hearty pink. "Pray forget I said that, Lord Wileham. It ought not to have been said."

"But at least I now know your true feelings about Lord Pleasanton," he told her, finding himself filled with relief by what she had, for Lord Pleasanton's attentions to her – and the knowledge that they were to walk together again – had been something which had burned hard into Andrew's thoughts over the last few days. "He is not a gentleman whom you would consider to be of particular merit, then?"

"After what he said to me, do you think that I would have regard for him?" Lady Carsington clicked her tongue and shook her head. "I was very grateful for your presence when I was walking with Lord Pleasanton that day. He spoke to me of my late husband and practically *demanded* to know if I was seeking to marry again, and then became insulted when I told him that such questions were much too forward, and that I considered him rude."

"I wonder, then, why you agreed to walk with him again?"

Lady Carsington's eyes pulled away from his and back towards the fire.

"Because he attempted to apologize," she answered, quietly. "And because I was... I was foolish." A soft smile curved her lips as she looked over to him again, her voice quieter now. "That is all I will say on the matter, however. I will admit to my foolishness and that is all. The truth is, as you now know, I have no interest in walking with Lord Pleasanton, or furthering my acquaintance with him, and I have no intention of doing so."

"I confess myself glad to hear it," he remarked, seeing her smile grow. "I do not think Lord Pleasanton is as excellent a fellow as he appears to be."

"Mayhap you are right."

"I am." With a confident grin, he chuckled when she laughed. "To my mind, Lady Carsington, you appear to be a lady who knows her own mind, and who is more than able to make any judgement necessary on the matter of gentlemen such as Lord Pleasanton."

"And what about you?" she asked, making his smile shatter. "Do you think that I am right in my judgements about you?"

The sudden solemnity of her question had his heart pounding in his chest to the point that he could not summon the words to answer her for some minutes. Lady Carsington simply lifted her eyebrow and waited, however, giving him no alternative but to respond to her.

"I – I do not know, Lady Carsington." The twisted tightness in his throat had his voice rasping. "What are your judgements about me?"

Lady Carsington paused for a short while, studying him with gentle eyes before she smiled.

"I think, Lord Wileham, that you are a gentleman who has long been pursuing his own temporary happiness without realizing the injury he has done by doing so."

The frown on Andrew's face grew.

"Injury?"

"The young ladies that you pursue, the ones whom you seek out simply so that they might admire you, seek you out and constantly hope to capture your attention, bear both pain and sorrow when you do not give them what they seek. You place yourself in their sphere but, once they are drawn to you, you turn away from them. Your part is over, your task has been completed and thus, you are contented. They, however, are left with longing, sadness, and a sense of regret about ever allowing themselves to be drawn to you in the first place." There was no hardness to her voice, no anger flickering in her eyes, but yet Andrew felt the sting of her gentle rebuke all the same. "Tell me, do you ever consider that?"

"Consider what I leave these young ladies with?" Wincing, he shook his head. "No, I have generally not done so. Lord Dorchester, however, has pointed out the same thing to me recently and, I will admit to you, Lady Carsington, that I have become all the more aware of my behavior of late. If I am to be honest, then I would say that I am considering it, attempting to view it in a fresh light."

Her eyes widened a little but when she smiled at him, it was as though the room suddenly glowed with a new brightness.

"I am glad to hear that, Lord Wileham."

"I find that my heart is all the more inclined towards *one* lady in particular," he found himself saying, "rather than being drawn to many."

Lady Carsington's smile persisted. It did not fade, but her eyes lingered on his, her head tilting a fraction.

"Is that so?"

"It is. It is a very strange state of affairs for me, Lady Carsington, for it is not a situation in which I have ever found myself before."

"And what do you intend to do about it?"

Andrew hesitated, then nodded – half to himself, half to her.

"I intend to simply consider it," he told her, quietly. "As I have said, this is a new situation for me, and I must do all that I can to understand it before I respond. Does that make sense to you, Lady Carsington?"

She nodded, her eyes never leaving his face.

"I think it a very wise idea. These matters of the heart are always worthy of a great deal of consideration, Lord Wileham."

"You sound as though you speak from some experience of such things."

A quiet, slightly sad laugh came from her as she shook her head.

"I did not love my late husband, and he did not love me. It was a match of suitability, and one I will always be grateful for – we were well suited, a contented match, and with much to like about each other. I will say that Lord Carsington was an excellent gentleman, who was kind, considerate, and eager to make sure that I was happy. We rubbed along very well together, and I do think that, perhaps in time, we might have come to feel something more than mere friendship for each other."

"The loss of him must have been painful for you."

"It was," she admitted, softly, looking away from him again, "but no, Lord Wileham, I do not have experience of matters of the heart. That being said, I have my own considerations at present, and I think time is always of the utmost importance."

When her eyes caught his, Andrew's breath hitched. There was hope there, a quiet sense of happiness building in his heart as he took her in again.

But he still had his truth to tell. He still had the explanation about the bet and the consequences to offer her and, when he did, would she continue to consider him in the same way?

~

"Good day, Lady Carsington. Allow me to express to you my deepest gratitude for what you have done for me." Lady Carsington smiled as they stood by the front door of her townhouse. The carriage was outside, waiting, but the door between Andrew and the carriage remained closed so that the cold winter air would not push its way unnecessarily into the house. He would open it to step outside and then close it tightly behind him again, leaving Lady Carsington inside and that, at the moment, seemed to be the most difficult thing of all to do. "I could have been gravely ill, had you not brought me back to your townhouse. Your kindness is something I value greatly and admire all the more."

"Enough, Lord Wileham," Lady Carsington laughed, settling one hand on his arm for a moment. "There is no need to continually express your gratitude. I would have done the same for anyone, whether they were a beggar or..." her eyes twinkled, her hands curling lightly around his arm, "or an Earl who had become lost in the snow."

"I have no intention of stepping out in the snow again," he promised her, reaching across with his other hand and settling it over her fingers as they rested on his arm. "I will openly admit to my foolishness – though I will say that the opportunity it brought me to be in your company for a prolonged duration is something which I am grateful for, in a way."

She laughed but did not pull her fingers away.

"I understand what you mean."

They stood together for a few moments, his hand on hers, her hand on his arm and, as he looked down into her face, the soft smile which had been gracing Lady Carsington's face began to fade away. It did not lead to a frown, however, but to something more, something Andrew could not quite make out. Was it desire? A hope that something would spark between them? He could feel the pull in his chest, the desire to move closer to her, to wrap his arms around her and lower his head, but the urge itself gave him pause. Yes, he had felt such a thing before with some of the other young ladies he had been pursuing, to the point that they sought him out in return, but never with this intensity, never with the swell of longing which currently roared through him. It was so strong, that Andrew did not think he could fight it and, really, he did not think he *would* fight it, even if he wished to.

"Lady Carsington – Julianna." Taking a deep breath, Andrew closed his eyes. The truth had to be spoken first before he could do anything else. "There is something I wish to tell you."

When he opened his eyes, Lady Carsington was looking up at him with wide eyes, her lips gently parted. With a quiet groan escaping from him, Andrew made to turn his head away, made to pull away from her before he did something he could not turn back from – but the next moment, she was in his arms, her hands at the nape of his neck and his mouth had found hers.

It was everything he wanted and everything he feared, all in one heady moment, and Andrew could not turn away from it. His heart was already crying out for more, begging him to linger, to stay with her wrapped in his arms, and the only thing he could do was obey.

CHAPTER FOURTEEN

"Goodness, I did not know if we would see each other again before Christmas Day! Indeed, I was concerned that you would not be able to join us for the day itself, and that would have been unthinkable!"

Julianna smiled and looped her arm through Lady Gilford's as they walked around Lord Hentley's ballroom.

"It would have been."

Her smile lingered as she thought of the last few days and all that had taken place. To find Lord Wileham in the snow and to aid him in his recovery had been difficult, and filled with a strain she had not expected, but what had come thereafter, once he had regained his strength, had been something quite different. She had not intended to kiss him, of course, but that had come out of her own desires and her inability to wait any longer. It had been a moment of recklessness, of acting on what she felt before giving herself any real consideration, but she did not regret it. When the kiss had ended, they had merely smiled at one another before Lord Wileham had taken his leave. No words had been shared, but perhaps there had not been the need to – each knew how the other felt and thus, their coming together had felt right. The battle in her heart and mind over him was no longer present. Lady Gilford had always told her that Lord Wileham had never done anything more than tease and flirt with a young lady but with her, he had not only pulled her tight against him, but they had also shared a long kiss which, she was sure, he had not done with any other young lady. Besides which, their conversations over the last few days – in particular, the ones regarding matters of the heart – had been honest and truthful. She had no doubt now that Lord Wileham had been struggling with the same sensations and desires as she had been. It was almost a relief to know that, for it meant that he was not about to turn around and laugh at her for her foolishness in permitting her heart to feel something for him, not when he shared her feelings.

"You are quite well, I hope? You were not too lonely in your townhouse this last sennight?" Lady Gilford glanced at her. "With Christmas only a sennight away, I do hope that we do not get any other great flurries of snow, otherwise I shall be most disappointed. I have the most marvelous feast arranged! It is all planned out most carefully and looked at everything in great detail, for what with the snow, I had the time to do so!"

"I am sure that the weather will listen to your concerns and do its utmost not to spoil them," Julianna replied, seeing Lady Gilford smile. "Do not worry, my friend. All will be well, I am sure."

"And you?" Lady Gilford asked, turning her head to look at Julianna again. "What did you do with your time during the last few days?"

Julianna hesitated.

"I – I had a guest."

"A guest?" The frown on Lady Gilford's face was easily

understandable and Julianna tried to smile, though suddenly nervous about sharing what had occurred with Lord Wileham. "How could you have a guest when there was so much snow outside? Hardly anyone could come and go and the carriages –"

"I found Lord Wileham on the road," Julianna interrupted, her words coming out in a rush. "He was almost frozen to the bone and fell into a dead faint when my coachman went to speak with him. I had no other choice but to take him to my townhouse and help him recover as best I could."

Lady Gilford's mouth fell open, and she let out such a loud exclamation that Julianna had to shush her quietly, only for Lady Gilford to harrumph and fold her arms across her chest.

"That gentleman will do anything he can to get your attention, Julianna," she stated, with a toss of her head. "I do hope that you were not taken in by him. How long did he stay for?"

"First of all, you *must* lower your voice," Julianna whispered, and Lady Gilford immediately ducked her head, a hint of color in her cheeks now. "I tell you this not because I want your judgement but because I simply must tell *someone*." She grasped her friend's hand and looked straight into her eyes. "Can I trust you with this?"

Lady Gilford nodded.

"Of course you can," she said, quietly. "Forgive me. I was overcome with surprise."

"Which I understand." Letting go of her hand, Julianna took a breath and then began to explain. She told Lady Gilford about what had happened at the carriage, the shock which had overwhelmed her when she had realized who it was, and what she had been required to do thereafter. Lady

Gilford's eyes grew wider and wider, astonishment flaring there until Julianna did not think that they could get any bigger. "Therefore, I do not think that the gentleman did anything purposefully, Marianne," she finished. "It was quite by accident that he found my carriage, and no one would make themselves so unwell simply because they wished to garner the attention of a lady!"

Lady Gilford nodded and looked away, her lips twisting to one side for a few moments, her brows lowered. Julianna remained quiet, waiting for her friend's response and, eventually, one came.

"I will concur that there can be no deliberate action there," Lady Gilford agreed eventually. "So he was present with you for three days?"

Julianna nodded.

"And he was not at all improper?"

"No, he was not." *But I was.* Fire licked up into her cheeks as she saw Lady Gilford's eyes narrow. "I like him, Marianne." Instantly, Lady Gilford closed her eyes. "I am aware of your warnings, and I agree with all of them," Julianna added, quickly, "but I also know that there is something between us which I cannot ignore."

"But that is what he *wants* you to believe," Lady Gilford hissed, putting one hand to Julianna's arm. "Do you not see? You have succumbed to him, just as every other young lady has done. He will turn his attentions away from you now, will leave you alone in your desires and will then look to another."

Julianna shook her head.

"I do not think so."

Lady Gilford closed her eyes and sighed, running one hand over her forehead.

"Pray, do not tell me that you believe there is something

of significance between you! You cannot be so foolish, Julianna. I have spoken to you of him, I have given you many warnings and now you do precisely the opposite of what I asked of you!"

"Perhaps because I do not see the difficulties you present."

Aware that every word she said seemed to only convince Lady Gilford that she was lost in foolishness, Julianna sighed and wondered silently if she ought not to have said anything at all.

"Do you think that he is suddenly going to turn around and ask to court you?" Lady Gilford threw up her hands. "I will admit that he has been eager to be in your company of late and yes, he even danced with you twice which he has never done before, but it is all just a show! You were not particularly eager for his company and now, after all he has done, and all the attention that he has shown you, you find yourself almost desperate for his company, just as he wanted. You have fallen for him, Julianna and now, no doubt rejoicing that he has succeeded, he will look to someone new."

"I do not believe that." The memory of their kiss had the fire in her cheeks burning all the hotter, but she gazed directly at her friend, steadily. "I think that there is something true between us and I will not let myself believe that he will turn from me. Not now. Not after what we have shared."

With a scowl, Lady Gilford turned herself away, looking out at the dance floor and gesturing to it.

"No doubt Lord Wileham is, at this present moment, dancing with any young lady he pleases and –"

"Lord Wileham has not been dancing with anyone."

A slightly mournful voice caught Julianna's attention

and, as she turned to look, she saw Lady Gilford's frown. A young lady stood just behind them, her gaze on the dance floor also, though she spoke directly to Lady Gilford.

"Forgive me for interrupting your conversation, but Lord Wileham has not been dancing with a single soul this last fortnight." Sighing heavily, she shook her head. "I thought he would be interested in my company but, thus far, he has only stepped out to dance with *you,* Lady Carsington."

A pair of blue, accusing eyes turned themselves towards Julianna and she recoiled a little.

"That was most considerate of Lord Wileham, I am sure, given that Lady Carsington has not been in society for some years."

Lady Gilford's tone was firm, and her eyes a little narrowed as she looked directly back at the young lady who continued to glare at Julianna.

"Why does he only dance with you?" the young lady asked, ice thick around her words. "Why do you walk with him in the park when he has never stepped out with anyone before?"

"I..."

Julianna blinked and tried to find a response, but none came. Helplessly, she looked at Lady Gilford. She did not even know this young lady's name, so how was she meant to address this?

"If you have any concern about Lord Wileham, Miss Jeffries, then might I suggest that you speak with *him* about it, rather than come to demand answers from Lady Carsington?" Lady Gilford took a step closer and finally, Miss Jeffries tore her eyes away from Julianna, letting her breathe a little more easily. "Lady Carsington knows none of what has gone before. To her, Lord Wileham is merely a charming gentleman, one among many others." Miss Jeffries sniffed, turned, and flounced away, leaving Julianna staring after her. "You see the effect that he has on all of these young ladies," Lady Gilford murmured, as Julianna swallowed the ache in her throat. "Lord Wileham is a gentleman who has charmed them all, but never taken one to his heart."

Julianna nodded and licked her lips.

"I understand that."

"Be careful he is not doing the same to you," Lady Gilford finished, reaching to grasp Julianna's hand tightly. "The last thing I want for you this Christmas is to have you nursing a broken heart."

∼

"A DANCE, LADY CARSINGTON?"

Julianna's heart leaped and she smiled as Lord Wileham beamed back at her, his expression one of pure happiness.

And then she remembered Miss Jeffries.

"Might I ask, Lord Wileham, who else it is that you are dancing with this evening?"

His smile slowly began to dim.

"I beg your pardon?"

"Who else are you to dance with this evening?" she asked again as Lord Wileham began to frown. "I have not seen you stand up as yet this evening."

"Perhaps I do not want to stand up with anyone else," came the reply.

Julianna's lips flattened together, a frown plucking at her forehead.

"I have had one young lady point this out to me, Lord

Wileham. You have only stood up with me of late and have not danced with any other."

A small step had him closer to her, his voice low and husky and sending a tingling across her skin.

"Mayhap you might be able to ascertain why such a thing could be, Lady Carsington?"

When she looked up into his face, when her gaze melded with his, her fears began to melt away and she let out a slow breath, remembering the kiss that they had shared.

"I might be able to do so, I suppose."

The edge of his lips quirked, a bright flash in his green eyes and Julianna's heart thundered in her chest as the urge to move closer to him still, even in front of everyone else, almost had her feet moving of their own accord. Steadying herself, she took the dance card from her wrist and handed it to him, watching his smile grow as he wrote his name in two spaces, with the latter being the supper dance.

"Whoever remarked about my dancing is quite right," he stated, as he handed her back her card, the brush of his fingers on hers making her jump. "I can only dance with you." Smiling at her, he tilted his head, studying her as though they had just met for the first time, and he wanted to recall her features. "And it is only you that I *wish* to dance with."

The worry in her heart began to fade as she smiled back at him, wishing that the dance would come a little more quickly so she might be in his arms again. There was so much to be said between them, so much for them to consider with respect to the future, but for the moment, she was happy simply to be in his company again.

"I find that I feel much the same way," she murmured, quietly. "I look forward to dancing with you again, Lord

Wileham, no matter what anyone else might have to say about it."

"Capital." Grinning, he bowed at the waist and then turned, offering his arm. "Mayhap you might wish for a turn about the room before the first of our dances, Lady Carsington? That is, if you have the time to spare?"

With a small, contented sigh, she took his arm and looked up at him, smiling.

"For you, Lord Wileham, I have all the time in the world."

CHAPTER FIFTEEN

The Christmas ball at Lord and Lady Richardson's was a spectacular affair, Andrew had to admit to himself. There was greenery everywhere, with holly berries adorning some wreaths which hung above the doors and the fireplace, reminding him of the one he had made with Lady Carsington. That made him smile, his heart quickening at the thought of seeing her again. Ever since he had awoken in her townhouse, things had changed completely. His heart, which still yearned for her, was given freedom to do so, and he now no longer found himself clinging to the hope of being admired and adored by all.

"You look... happy. And yet, there is not a young lady in sight!" Lord Arthington appeared out of the crowd and slapped Andrew on the shoulder. "Whatever happened to you that night we went gambling? You threw your cards down and, thereafter, I did not see you again!"

"And you did not think to come looking for me? You did not pause and think that you should, mayhap, send a note?"

"The snow was *very* severe," Lord Arthington reminded

him, though he did not look in Andrew's direction, a hint of color splashing across his face. "I could not send anyone."

Andrew arched an eyebrow questioningly. It had been some days since the dreadful snowfall and he had been able to send plenty of notes and take his carriage to a good number of places, which meant that Lord Arthington could not use the snow as an excuse. His words fell back into his mind, however, rather than be spoken, for he saw that it was not worth pursuing. He was beginning to understand that the gentlemen he had chosen for his friends were not perhaps the sort of gentlemen he wished to have as companions any longer. Lord Dorchester was the exception, of course, for he had been the first to step away in pursuit of marriage but now, with Andrew close to following in his stead, that left men like Lord Arthington a little further behind.

Looking at his friend, Andrew considered all that had passed between them these last few weeks. Lord Arthington had not shown any true concern over Andrew's absence from the gambling den, had spoken out of turn on more than one occasion, and could not truly be relied on for anything. He liked to have fun, to tease and mortify where he could. Was that the sort of companion Andrew wanted?

"Your happiness has dissipated a little, I think." Lord Arthington grinned. "Perhaps I am not the company you hoped for."

"No, you are not." Andrew lifted his chin and looked Lord Arthington straight in the eye. "Arthington, I have come to my senses at last."

"Oh?"

Andrew nodded, half to himself, half to Lord Arthington.

"I have decided that I no longer wish to behave as I have done these last few years."

Lord Arthington snorted.

"Is that so?"

"It is." With a deep breath, Andrew let his lungs fill with air and looked around the room again, as if he were seeing it for the very first time. "I have no desire to dance with young ladies simply to pull away from them thereafter. I do not want their smiles, their accolades, their sighs of discontent when I move away from them."

"I can hardly believe that to be true!" Lord Arthington threw up his hands, then let them fall, a guffaw escaping him. "You are jesting."

"I am not." With as much firmness as he could – and growing a little irritated at Lord Arthington's demeanor – he folded his arms over his chest. "I have decided to change my ways."

Even this did not seem to convince Lord Arthington, for he shook his head firmly, his grin still broad across his face.

"You say such things only to annoy me, I know. You cannot have altered that much."

Andrew let his smile grow, albeit a little grimly.

"And what if I have? What if I have decided that this is no longer to be the path I take?"

Finally, Lord Arthington's smile began to fade.

"Then you will follow Dorchester?" he asked, his tone disbelieving. "You will decide to settle upon one young lady and pursue her for the rest of your days?"

"And what if I do?" Andrew shrugged. "It cannot be so bad a future, Arthington. I have discovered more these last few weeks in terms of happiness and contentment than I have the last three years!"

At this, Lord Arthington frowned, his brows low over

his eyes and a shadow etching itself across his features.

"That is ridiculous. You have enjoyed the last few years... as have I."

"If you wish to continue as you have always done, then do not permit my change of mind to force your steps along another path," Andrew answered, refusing to take offence at Lord Arthington's remarks. "I make this decision in the full understanding of what it will do, as regards our friendship, but nonetheless, it is something I must do."

"Must?" Lord Arthington snorted. "I did not think you a weak-willed man, Wileham, and yet here you are, following Dorchester simply because he has gained a little more respectability through his connection with Miss Hallstrom. You do not *need* respectability, Wileham. You are perfectly contented just as you are, I know it! You are 'the uncatchable gentleman', the one that captures the heart of almost every young lady in London, each hoping that *they* will be the one to steal him away. Why should you want to change that?"

"Because I do not want to be 'the uncatchable gentleman', and thus be perpetually pursued! I am tired of all of this!"

Lord Arthington's jaw tightened.

"What are you tired of, pray tell? Tired of your friends? The evenings at White's, the dancing, the carousing – though you have never engaged in such a thing as that." A small, sly smile passed across his face. "Mayhap if you *did* join me in such adventures, you might find this idea of becoming a different sort of gentleman to be an utterly ridiculous one."

Andrew's stomach roiled, his hands rolling into tight fists.

"Enough, Arthington."

"*That* is what you need!" Lord Arthington seemed to ignore him, slapping him on the shoulder again as Andrew gritted his teeth. "You need to bed the lady, that is all. She is a widow, so it will not cause any great consternation! Do that and then forget about her! Move onto the next entertainment, just as *I* do. Then, I can assure you, you will be satisfied and content."

Andrew's heart began to beat furiously, anger stirring up like a violent sea.

"The last thing I want to do is become anything like you."

He did not recoil upon saying these words, did not immediately apologize or beg his friend's apology. Instead, with fury boiling in his veins, he twisted away from Lord Arthington and marched across the room, refusing to linger in his company for another moment, for fear of what he himself might do.

The thought of taking things further with Lady Carsington, only to then discard her, was almost painful for him to consider. With every muscle burning, every part of him on fire with anger, Andrew stalked across the room and then pushed open the French doors so that he could step outside. He would have to quieten his temper, regain his composure and, thereafter, make himself ready to enjoy the rest of the evening – hopefully in Lady Carsington's company.

~

"Our second – and final – dance of the evening, Lady Carsington."

Andrew smiled as Lady Carsington's cheeks warmed as she took his hand. Her smile was bright, and surely must be an indication of her high spirits, for who could not be enjoying themselves at this ball? There had been excellent wine served, not the usual watered wine which many a gentleman served, alongside the most delicious foods which were continually served in the dining room for those who wished to partake. There had been much music, dancing, and a good deal of merriment - and Andrew had enjoyed almost every moment. After his discussion and subsequent ending of the connection between himself and Lord Arthington, he had composed himself and then chosen to forget about what had been said, in favor of the time he could then spend with Lady Carsington instead. Now that he was walking with her to the center of the ballroom, knowing that there was a mistletoe bough near them, his heart was leaping about his chest as his anticipation grew steadily. There had not been a single moment where he had considered someone else, where he had even *looked* at another lady. Instead, there had only been Lady Carsington in his view, in his thoughts and now, on his arm.

"We are to dance, Lady Carsington."

Smiling, he bowed and then stepped to take her into his arms, the waltz beginning to swell around them. Their steps moved in unison and Andrew danced with ease, delighting in every moment that he had to hold her close.

The mistletoe bough hung above them and, slowing, Andrew reached up to pluck one but, much to his surprise, Lady Carsington was the one to do so before he could even touch the berries.

"You have our mistletoe berry, Lady Carsington," he murmured, as the other dancers continued to move around them. "I believe it must be exchanged for a kiss."

"Then I shall keep it," she told him, with a small, slightly coy smile. "Until a time of *my* choosing."

The anticipation poured thought him and he snatched

in a breath, barely able to contain himself from dropping his head and kissing her right then and there. The twinkle in her eye told him that she was thinking much the same thing and, with a breath to steady himself, Andrew took her hand in his and began to waltz again.

"There is much that we need to discuss, Lady Carsington," he murmured, as they continued around the room. "I do not want you to think that I am unaware of this connection between us."

"I am also very aware of it," she answered, her hand tightening in his. "I should be glad of the opportunity to talk with you about it all."

Andrew smiled at her, aware of just how full his heart had become – and how glad he was for it all.

"Our connection means a great deal to me, Lady Carsington... Julianna."

Her eyes closed for a moment, and she let out a slow breath, smiling back at him.

"As it does to me, Lord Wileham."

There was no opportunity for anything more to be said, for the music began to slow and soon, they were forced to step apart. Bowing to her, Andrew offered her his arm again and together, they walked back towards the side of the ballroom. To his surprise, he saw Lord Dorchester waiting for him, his face black with obvious anger. Jaw tight, eyes narrowed, he stepped forward as Andrew reached the edge of the ballroom, though Andrew released Lady Carsington's arm at once. Turning to her, he caught the concern in her eyes and tried to smile.

"Pray, excuse me, Lady Carsington."

She nodded.

"But of course."

Stepping to his friend, Andrew regarded him carefully.

"Lord Dorchester, whatever is the matter? You look as though —"

"How could you?" Lord Dorchester hissed, as Andrew grabbed his arm and tugged him away from the crowd, back towards the French doors. "Remove your hands from me!"

"Whatever this is, do not cause an upset in the middle of the ball," Andrew warned, his heart beginning to hammer hard in his chest. "It would not be fair."

"You speak of fair?" Lord Dorchester threw off Andrew's restraining hand again, his eyes blazing with fury. "After everything I asked of you, after all the assurances you gave me, you chose to ignore it all and go directly back to *her*?"

"Her?" Andrew blinked, then shook his head as they stood by the French doors, the cold air filling the space between them. "Dorchester, I have not even the smallest iota of understanding of this matter. Whatever has taken place, I can assure you, it is not by my hand."

Lord Dorchester let out such a cry of rage that Andrew stumbled back, losing his balance completely. With the French doors open, there was no wall to protect him from his fall and thus, he landed hard on his back on the cold stone with snow whispering down over him. Lord Dorchester did not seem to care, for he immediately strode to where he lay, standing over him, eyes dark with wrath, arms wide as he gesticulated furiously.

"I *told* you to stay away from Miss Hallstrom — and then Lord Arthington tells me that this very evening, you went to attempt to pull her into your arms! What were you thinking? How could you treat our friendship with such disdain? I understand that you are angry about the bet and the consequences which followed — though you appear to be perfectly contented with only Lady Carsington's company

– but to be so cruel, so *unfeeling* is utterly despicable." His arms fell to his sides, and he kicked out hard and Andrew cried out in pain as his friend's foot connected with his ribs. "I should call you out, defend my Lady's honor but you are not worth the price of a bullet."

So saying, he swung around and walked straight back inside. Andrew groaned again, his hands clutching at his chest where Lord Dorchester's foot had kicked him, trying to make sense of all that had been said only for another voice to break through the haze of pain.

"The bet?"

Immediately, scrabbling to push himself up, Andrew reached out into the gloom to grab Lady Carsington's hand, but she backed away from him at once, her eyes wide as moonlight illuminated her features.

"Yes, there was a bet, but that is not important now. Not after what I have learned about myself, not now that my heart is –"

"Then it is all a lie." Lady Carsington stared at him, then closed her eyes, her expression crumpling. "Marianne was right." Her voice fell to a tortured whisper. "I have been nothing but a fool."

"No, Julianna, no!" Reaching for her again, he fought to get to his feet, his chest heaving, agony spreading out across his chest. "I meant every word I have said to you thus far. My intention to speak with you about my feelings is honest! I –"

Lady Carsington covered her face with her hands and, with a strangled sob, turned away from him and fled back into the ballroom. Andrew went to follow her but the pain in his ribs made it near impossible to do so. Stumbling, he grasped at something – anything – to hold onto, but Lady Carsington was already gone.

CHAPTER SIXTEEN

"Keep your head high." Lady Thurston slipped her arm through Julianna's as they walked through Lord Umbridge's drawing room. "Recall, no one else knows of what took place between yourself and Lord Wileham, save for Lady Gilford and I."

"And I am grateful to both of you for your friendship, and the trust which I have in you to keep such things to yourself." Julianna sniffed and swallowed the tears which threatened. "I do not want to be here this evening, however. I think mayhap, I shall return home soon."

"That would be the very worst thing for you to do," Lady Gilford stated, firmly. "You must not allow this to push you from society. People would then ask questions about *why* you were absent, and that might lead to rumors. Recall, the *ton* are aware that Lord Wileham has been showing you particular attention. We do not want there to be any whispers."

Julianna wanted to say that she did not care in the least if any whispers came but, instead, fell silent. Her friends were doing all that they could to protect her, and she appreciated that a great deal, even if she was weary, broken-hearted, and aching about what had taken place.

Hearing only a little of what Lord Dorchester had thrown at Lord Wileham had been enough for her to realize that Lady Gilford had spoken the truth. Lord Wileham was *not* the gentleman she had thought him to be. Instead, he had used his wiles to encourage her affections while, at the same time it seemed, paying attention to another young lady as well. She had not deliberately come to overhear what had been said between the two gentlemen. When she had seen Lord Wileham fall backwards through the open French doors, had found herself hurrying towards him for fear of what had happened – and then Lord Dorchester had spoken those terrible words which had torn pieces out of her soul.

She was dull now, and lifeless. All that she had shared with Lord Wileham was nothing but falsehoods and pretense. Even the time that they had made wreaths together had, no doubt, been carefully calculated by him so that she would feel herself drawn to him, would see his change in manner and would be pleased that she had helped encourage it.

She had been a complete and utter fool.

"Ah, Lady Carsington!"

Stopping, Julianna dropped into a curtsey, sighing as she rose.

"Lord Pleasanton."

"We did not get our walk together." Lord Pleasanton smiled briefly, ignoring both Lady Thurston and Lady Gilford. "The weather was too terrible for me even to get a note to you!"

Realizing with a start that she had quite forgotten about her second outing with Lord Pleasanton and had not even noticed the supposed date for it passing her by, Julianna forced a smile.

"I quite understand."

"Mayhap we might arrange another time?"

The hope in his eyes had her heart sinking.

"Lord Pleasanton, if you wish to walk with me so that we might make amends, then I should be glad to. If, however, you hope that I will have changed my mind and have now decided that yes, I *shall* marry you, then I must disabuse you of such thoughts at once."

Lord Pleasanton's smile began to crack.

"I had hoped to walk with you, Lady Carsington, that is all. After all, it was *you* who suggested we walk together."

"And I did so because I wanted to make such an arrangement in front of Lord Wileham," she stated, hearing Lady Thurston's catch of breath, but finding that she did not care about insulting the gentleman. The only thing she wanted to do at present was to be truthful. "I have no interest in your company, Lord Pleasanton. I do not want to improve our connection, I have no thought of courtship, betrothal or the like, and would be very eager indeed to make certain that you understand my thinking in this." Lord Pleasanton's face went a shade reminiscent of parchment and, for some moments, he opened and closed his mouth as though he wanted to find something to say in response, but could not think of what his response should be. "I do not think that we require another walk together, do you?" Julianna finished, wearily. "Good evening, Lord Pleasanton. I wish you every success in finding a suitable young lady to marry. I, however, shall not be her."

With this, she moved away and left Lady Gilford to choke out a few words of farewell before turning and making her way after Julianna.

"Whatever were you thinking?"

"I was thinking that I needed to be truthful," Julianna replied, seeing her friend's wide eyes, but feeling nothing but relief within her own heart. "I spoke foolishly when I was last in Lord Pleasanton's company and mayhap gave him the impression that what I had said earlier was no longer the case. I wished to clarify that."

"Well, you certainly did that!" Lady Gilford exclaimed, her eyes still rounded. "Good gracious, I do not think anyone has ever spoken to Lord Pleasanton in such a way before."

Julianna tried to smile, but her mouth did not lift. Instead, her brow furrowed, and heat built behind her eyes, though she did not let any tears spark into her vision. She could not lose her composure here, not when there were so many others present.

"You are not yourself, and I am sorry for that." Lady Gilford slipped an arm through Julianna's again. "I do not like seeing the pain within you, my dear friend."

"I do not like feeling it." Julianna sighed and closed her eyes briefly. "I do not like that I was nothing but an imbecile in believing Lord Wileham's words and expressions. When he kissed me, I felt sure that –"

"He kissed you?" Lady Gilford hissed in surprise, turning swiftly so that she faced Julianna. "When? With the mistletoe?"

Julianna dropped her gaze to the floor, miserable as she recalled the moment that she had touched her lips to his.

"In truth, it was not he who kissed me but I who kissed him," she answered, brokenly, glad that they were in a quiet corner and so could not be overheard. "He was taking his leave from my house and then... well, we shared a sweet moment and thereafter, he went to his carriage."

Lady Gilford, rather than exclaiming that this was ridiculous and asking Julianna what she could have been thinking by doing such a thing, simply tilted her head and frowned.

"But he continued to pursue you thereafter."

Julianna glanced up at her friend.

"What do you mean?"

"He sought you out to dance with," Lady Gilford said, slowly. "There was another mistletoe bough."

"Yes, but we know that it was not out of desire to be in my company but from duty," Julianna reminded her, her heart squeezing with a fresh, sharp pain. "That is what Lord Dorchester said. It was nothing but a pretense."

Lady Gilford hesitated, then looked away.

"I suppose."

"You ought to be agreeing with me in this!" Julianna exclaimed, quickly lowering her voice again so as not to gain attention. "I told you what was said, I told you of his defense, the words he threw at me in desperation – clearly still eager for me to believe him, to trust that his desire for me was genuine - but I could not accept a single word from him, not after realizing what it was that he had done."

"But what if there was some truth in it?"

Julianna's mouth fell open, a sense of betrayal beginning to bite at her.

"How can you even suggest such a thing, Marianne? You were the one who warned me from him."

"Yes, but you shared a kiss with him," Lady Gilford explained, putting her hands out either side, "and thereafter, he still pursued you."

"Because he *had* to."

"Did he?" Lady Gilford tilted her head. "He had already garnered your affection, your interest in him. He could have simply stayed away from *all* ladies for the duration of the Christmas season – yourself included – but instead, he continued to draw close to you. Do you not understand, Julianna? With every other young lady that he has pursued, Lord Wileham has captured their heart and then immediately moved to speak with and interact with someone new. If he has captured you, then why did he not move away? Yes, it may be that he was not permitted by this bet – whatever it was – to tease any other young ladies – but should he not have then stepped away from you, just as he has done many times before?"

Julianna shook her head, a buzzing in her ears.

"I do not think that makes sense, Marianne. He was bound by this bet to be in my company and my company alone."

"But once he had caught your interest, he would have wanted to push you away from him, not pull you closer," Lady Gilford said, slowly, as though she were still trying to make sense of it all within her own thoughts. "I think there may be something more here, Julianna."

Julianna closed her eyes, her breathing a little quickened, her hands curling into tight fists so that she could keep hold of her composure.

"My dear friend, you cannot say such things. My heart is already broken; my pain is already significant enough without more being placed upon it."

"I do not mean to add to your injuries." Quickly, Lady Gilford grasped Julianna's hands, her eyes searching her face. "I mean to give you a little hope, actually."

"Hope?" Julianna laughed bitterly. "I do not have any hope. I have been a fool, heedless of your warnings and letting go of my own sensible thoughts to pursue what felt wonderful." Her head dropped as she battled fresh tears. "I was close to falling in love with him, Marianne. Perhaps... perhaps I should never have come to London."

"Do not say such a thing!" Lady Gilford's voice was filled with tears now, but Julianna could not bring herself to lift her head. "I have been glad of your company, and though there have been some trials, there is still happiness here. There can still *be* happiness, my dear Julianna. There is Christmas Day still to come, with Christmas dinner and gifts for you waiting on my parlor table." She took a deep breath and grasped Julianna's hand in hers. "We will make this a happier Christmas than you expect, even with everything that has happened."

Julianna nodded, and tried to believe what Lady Gilford was saying, but her heart would not let her. Too full of agonies and regrets, it pulled her down and even as she lifted her head and forced a wobbly smile, Julianna felt nothing but darkness settling within her.

Lord Wileham had stolen all of the light and happiness from her, and now she did not know how she was ever to get it back again.

CHAPTER SEVENTEEN

*A*ndrew groaned and pinched the bridge of his nose with one hand, crumpling up the paper into a ball and then flinging it in the direction of the fire. It had been four days since the incident with Lord Dorchester and thus far, he had not found a way to explain himself to Lady Carsington. He had been forced to rest on the first day, given the bruising to his ribs, but thereafter, had found himself desperate to write to her, wanting nothing more than to explain himself, but everything he wrote sounded either like a justification, or came out as complete waffle. He was beginning to run out of patience with himself as well as running out of paper and still, his desperation grew.

Whatever was he to do? The ache in his heart came solely from his separation from Lady Carsington and yet, it was a separation that he deserved. To be near to her, to have that same closeness as they had built together was not something he could simply return to, not when he had behaved in this manner towards her. Yes, what Lord Dorchester had said of him was quite untrue, for he had never *once* gone near Miss Hallstrom but thereafter, what he had said of the bet and the consequences Andrew had faced because of it had been quite true. Only Lady Carsington had not heard him speak of his own heart and how it had been affected by her, about how it was no longer about the bet but rather because he wanted to be in her company - wanted it so much that this separation felt almost unbearable. It was like a physical pain that he could not part from himself, a wound that would never recover. Quite how he was to help it heal, Andrew did not know. Mayhap this was to be a thorn he would have to bear for the rest of his life and, mayhap, he would be grateful for it, if that was to be the case, for it would serve as a reminder of how foolish he had once been.

A tap came at the door and Andrew lifted his head from the back of the chair.

"Yes?"

The butler came in.

"My Lord, Lord Dorchester and Lord Arthington are in the parlor."

Andrew sat up straight.

"I beg your pardon?"

The butler repeated himself.

"Lord Arthington and Lord Dorchester have called, my Lord, and I set them in the parlor. I hope I did not do the wrong thing?"

"No, no, not in the least." Andrew's mind began to flood with a flurry of questions about why his two friends – or former friends – had come to call. "The parlor, you say?"

The butler nodded.

"A tray, my Lord? Shall I send one up?"

Andrew shook his head and pushed himself out of his chair, wincing a little at the pain in his side as he did so.

"No. Do not have anyone interrupt us." He did not

know why both gentlemen had called together, but there must be something of significance in their meeting. It was certainly *not* for a social occasion, not since Andrew had behaved so very poorly with Lord Arthington, and Lord Dorchester had railed at Andrew so furiously, so whatever could it be for?

Straightening his shoulders, Andrew fought back the wave of nervousness threatening to crash over him and, with a nod to himself, walked out of his study and made his way directly to the parlor. Putting one hand to the door, he drew in another breath and then, steeling himself for fear that fists might connect with him the moment that he opened the door, he stepped inside.

"Lord Arthington. Lord Dorchester."

Speaking with an unfamiliar formality to his two friends, Andrew nodded to them each in turn, noting how Lord Arthington quickly dropped his gaze to the floor, though Lord Dorchester came over towards Andrew directly and, much to his surprise, put one hand on his shoulder and looked directly at him.

"My sincerest apologies, Wileham."

Relief had Andrew's shoulders sinking, as the tension left them.

"Apologies?"

"For thinking that you had gone near Miss Hallstrom," Lord Dorchester said, throwing a glance at Lord Arthington. "Forgive me. I spoke to Miss Hallstrom the day after our... conversation... and she knew nothing of what I had been told."

Andrew nodded slowly, finding himself lost in confusion.

"You know, then, that I did not go near Miss Hallstrom? I did not dance or flirt with her, nor tease her. In fact, I do not think that I have even had the opportunity to converse with her in any way, since the day that you asked me to stay far from her."

Lord Dorchester nodded.

"I do understand that. And I believe your every word."

"That is good, at least." Still struggling to understand the dynamic between Lord Dorchester and Lord Arthington, given that Lord Arthington had the stance of a man who had been deeply shamed in some way, Andrew gripped Lord Dorchester's hand and shook it firmly. "You have revealed a great deal to me, Dorchester. I speak honestly in this matter, for I have not only seen the foolishness of my ways, but I have begun to realize what it is that you spoke of, when you told me about the happiness which one can find when in the constant, steady presence of only one lady." He released Lord Dorchester's hand. "When you first told me, I thought it laughable. Now, however, I can understand it. I have found myself with a great and deep affection for Lady Carsington and, to be frank, the thought of returning to the gentleman I was, the one who sought out affection and interest from as many ladies as he could, while refusing to share his heart with anyone, is something that fills me with disgust."

Lord Dorchester's lips quirked.

"I am glad to hear it." The smile flattened quickly. "And for my part, I am sorry for the physical injury which I placed on your person. I was lost in anger, furious over what I thought you had done – and I was afraid that Miss Hallstrom was not the person I had thought her. She and I share an affection for each other and, in truth, I became afraid that she had not told me the truth, but was only saying the same words as I, out of fear that I might turn from her otherwise."

Andrew put one hand to his heart.

"There is nothing to forgive, Dorchester. I can understand your anger – and I can also understand your belief that I had done such a thing. After all, it is not as though I am, based on past history, a gentleman of good character who has done what is best for others, rather than what is best for himself!" A wry smile tilted his mouth. "But I am endeavoring to be much improved now, I confess it." His gaze slid to Lord Arthington. "Arthington? Is there a reason for your presence here?"

"There is." It was not Lord Arthington who spoke, but rather Lord Dorchester, who immediately scowled and flung out one hand towards Lord Arthington. "Should you wish to tell him, Arthington? Or will I do the honors?"

Lord Arthington grimaced and sat down heavily into a chair, flinging out one hand towards Lord Dorchester which both Andrew and Lord Dorchester took to mean the same thing.

"Then I am to tell you," Lord Dorchester continued, with a shake of his head. "Shall we sit?"

"Please."

As Lord Dorchester sat down, Andrew poured three small measures of brandy and handed one to Lord Dorchester and one to Lord Arthington, though the latter refused his, so Andrew set it on a side table instead. Then he sat down himself, his gaze flicking from one person to the other, wondering what Lord Arthington had to do with all of this.

"On the evening in question, I went in search of you before I had given myself the opportunity to speak to Miss Hallstrom." With a sigh, Lord Dorchester shook his head. "Mayhap if I had been wise and spoken to her first, then none of this would have happened." Another breath and he closed his eyes, leaving Andrew to wonder what would come next. "The accusations I leveled at you, Wileham, did not come from Miss Hallstrom, given that she had no knowledge of what I was talking about. When I spoke to her of them, she told me that she had never heard of such a thing before, that you had *not* come near her, and certainly had not flirted or teased her either! She assured me of her affection for me and promised that she would always be loyal. I could see the pain in her expression because of what I had laid upon her, and my heart broke a little. I should have trusted her. I should have trusted what we share, but I did not."

"You did not trust me," Andrew said, as Lord Dorchester nodded, his eyes on his glass. "That is understandable."

"Perhaps." Lord Dorchester took another breath and threw a dark look towards Lord Arthington, and it was then, before he had even begun his explanations, that everything began to slot itself together inside Andrew's head. "Lord Arthington came to me that evening and told me that he had seen you with Miss Hallstrom."

Andrew's gaze shot towards Lord Arthington, his chest growing tighter with every breath.

"He told me specifically that, on that very evening, he had been with you, and you had told him of your intention to try to pull Miss Hallstrom into your embrace, to try to coerce her into offering you even a hint of interest. He said that you had no desire to break us apart, but that you could not be contented with my demands that you stay far from her."

Shaking his head, Andrew let out a slow breath.

"I said none of that. The only part of that which is true,

is the part about me having no wish to break you apart from Miss Hallstrom."

"I see that now," Lord Dorchester answered, with a scowl. "Lord Arthington decided, for whatever reason, to fill my head with lies and I, unfortunately, believed every word without even considering whether or not it was true."

"Why would you question it?" Andrew shrugged, then smiled ruefully. "It makes perfect sense to me that you would accept Lord Arthington's words... my only question, Arthington, is why you had cause to do such a thing?"

Lord Arthington's scowl remained fastened to his features.

"I was insulted."

Andrew closed his eyes, letting out a heavy breath.

"This is because of what I said to you."

"What was said?" Lord Dorchester glanced from Andrew to Lord Arthington and back again. "I am oblivious to all of this, and Lord Arthington would not give me his reasons for being so devious, so I am quite in the dark!"

Gesturing to Lord Arthington, Andrew began his explanation.

"I told Lord Arthington that I had no wish to continue on in my previous ways. I said that, in being forced to set all of my efforts on Lady Carsington, I had begun to realize what *you* had expressed, in finding happiness – a greater, more fulfilling happiness than I had ever expected – simply from being in her company. Lord Arthington did not find my words to be genuine and was inclined towards mockery. He told me that I ought to simply bed Lady Carsington and then move on, for *that* was what I was lacking." Heat flared in his chest, but he doused it quickly. "I lost my temper, for my feelings for Lady Carsington are greater than I had ever anticipated, and I found myself angry with Lord Arthington for speaking so callously of her. Therefore, I spoke harshly, and walked away before I could inflict anything further upon him!"

Lord Dorchester's expression cleared.

"And that is why you came and spoke to me about him," he said, turning back to Lord Arthington, whose head was now so low, his chin rested on his chest. "You lied so that there would be a great deal of pain inflicted upon Lord Wileham, in retaliation for what he had said to you." The silence which came from Lord Arthington was the only confirmation the men received, and Lord Dorchester blew out a long breath and shook his head in clear disbelief as Andrew sat back in his chair and took a sip of his brandy. Finally, it all became clear – but the damage had been done. "I am sorry it has taken me a few days to come to you with this, Wileham." Lord Dorchester's voice was dark. "I should have spoken to you earlier, but I wanted to make sure that my temper was not about to flare again, albeit not with you! And I demanded that Lord Arthington join me for, once Miss Hallstrom told me that she had no knowledge of what I was speaking about, and that you had not done anything of the sort, I realized that Lord Arthington had lied to me – and I confronted him with it. Thereafter, we came here."

"Do not apologize. You have done nothing wrong." Andrew narrowed his gaze in Lord Arthington's direction, his jaw flexing with a sudden anger. "Do you know what you have done, Arthington? Yes, you may have caused difficulties between me and Lord Dorchester which, thankfully, have been resolved, but you have broken apart myself and Lady Carsington. Mayhap that does not mean a great deal to you, mayhap you do not care, but I can assure you that the pain is very great indeed." Lord Arthington mumbled something incoherent, but Andrew did not ask him to repeat it. Whatever it was that Lord Arthington was trying to say, Andrew did not think it would bear any significance. Lord Arthington was a shallow character, who did not care for anyone but himself and, even if he apologized, Andrew did not think it would be genuine. "I am glad to know the truth, at least, and I hope that our connection is repaired?" Looking at Lord Dorchester, he smiled when his friend nodded. "This new path which I am on, the one I have been walking ever since I was forced in Lady Carsington's direction, has been one of the happiest – though most confusing – that I have ever been on. I am grateful for that and to you for your harsh words, though I did not appreciate them at the time!"

Lord Dorchester chuckled somewhat darkly, his brows low over his eyes.

"I am sorry for what I did in reacting so fiercely," he stated, with a growl in Lord Arthington's direction. "And with regard to Lady Carsington, mayhap there is something which can be done in order to absolve you a little?"

Andrew ran one hand down his face, recalling the agony in her voice when she had spoken to him as he lay on the cold, wet ground.

"I have been trying to write to her for the last three days, but nothing has come to mind. Part of what she heard is true and though the other is not, I do not know how to explain that."

"Then let me do so," Lord Dorchester said, quickly. "It is the least I can do, after the injury I delivered to your person."

Andrew took a deep breath and tried to find a flicker of hope in his heart that he might soon be returned to Lady Carsington's company, but nothing came.

"If you think that it would make a difference, then I will

not tell you to refrain, but I confess to you that I do not have any hope in that regard. I have broken her heart completely, and perhaps it cannot be mended."

"And perhaps it can," Lord Dorchester said, firmly. "I can only try."

Nodding, Andrew looked at him.

"When will you do so? Christmas is only two days from now!"

"Then tomorrow." A light came into his eyes. "You are to come to the Christmas soiree at Lord and Lady Cameron's townhouse, are you not? They are to have singing, entertainment and the like and I am certain that Lady Carsington will have been invited."

"I shall be in attendance." It had been his intention not to go to the soiree, but since there was hope that not only would Lady Carsington be there, but that Lord Dorchester would speak to her and explain some of his actions, Andrew resolved to make certain that he was present. "Thank you, Dorchester, for coming to explain this to me. I appreciate your honesty a great deal."

Lord Dorchester nodded and, though Andrew looked to Lord Arthington, the man said nothing. With a heaviness in his heart he had not expected, Andrew shrugged – half to himself – and then let his gaze go to the fire in the grate by Lord Dorchester's chair as his thoughts ran in turmoil through his mind. Would Lady Carsington be willing to listen to Lord Dorchester? And if she was, then could he permit himself to hope that she might, in time, come to forgive him for what he had kept back from her?

I think I am in love with her, his heart whispered, as his eyes lingered on the flames in the grate. *And I do not know what I am to do about it.*

CHAPTER EIGHTEEN

"This is *sure* to lift your spirits."

Julianna looked all around her, sniffing gently as she took in the delicate scent of pine which flooded the ballroom.

"It is certainly a wonderful atmosphere," she agreed, looking around and smiling gently.

There were candles on every surface, a roaring fire at one end of the ballroom and, everywhere she looked, there was holly, pine branches, mistletoe and other greenery strewn across the walls and in wreaths above the fireplace. There was laughter, and music was gently wafting towards her from the other end of the ballroom and, as Julianna took it all in, she found her heart lifting free of the pain and disappointment it had clung to for the last few days.

"It is good to see you smile," Lady Thurston murmured, as Lady Gilford nodded fervently. "You say that you have not seen Lord Wileham since the night of the ball?" Julianna shook her head, the happiness evaporating at the name of Lord Wileham on Lady Thurston's lips. "Perhaps he will be here this evening but, if he is to be present, then we shall make certain to take you far from him. Have no fear, my dear Julianna, we are beside you, and ready to protect you, so that you will have nothing but enjoyment and peace this evening."

"I appreciate your kindness, both of you." Julianna smiled and looked from Lady Thurston to Lady Gilford. "But you have husbands of your own, and I am sure that they will require your presence and your company also."

Lady Thurston laughed and shook her head.

"My dear husband is already in the card room."

"As is mine," Lady Gilford added, though she smiled and did not seem at all disappointed. "So we are to be with you for the entirety of the evening, if you wish it."

A settling relief poured into Julianna's veins, and she nodded quickly.

"Thank you."

"Now come, there is a lot to see, and a good many people to converse with. Before you know it, you will have forgotten all about Lord Wileham, I am sure."

Keeping her smile on her face, Julianna let her friends lead her across the ballroom, silently hoping that they were right. This Christmas, she was sure that she would still be nursing a broken heart and, though she could smile, laugh, and find some happiness in the various entertainments, that heavy weight would still continually pull her heart low.

"Lady Carsington?"

She turned, only to take a step back as Lord Dorchester, the gentleman who had thrown such anger at Lord Wileham – though justifiably, Julianna considered – bowed towards her.

"Lord Dorchester." She swallowed and glanced at her friends. "I am sure that you are already acquainted with Lady Thurston and Lady Gilford."

"I am, and good evening. Might I be so rude, however, as to steal you away for a few minutes?"

Julianna hesitated, seeing his eyes searching her face for an answer, but she had not yet decided what it was she ought to say.

"Might I ask, Lord Dorchester, what it is that you wish to speak about?"

"To be frank, it is about the exchange you witnessed between myself and Lord Wileham."

Shaking her head, Julianna held up one hand, palm out to him.

"Then if that is what you wish to speak about with me, I am afraid I must refuse you. I have no desire to hear any more."

Lord Dorchester frowned.

"My dear Lady, I do not know what it is that you overheard exactly, but the reason I wish to speak with you is because not all that I said to him was true. In fact, it has been made quite plain to me that almost everything I said did not have any real truth to it."

Julianna's heart leaped, but she quietened it quickly enough. She had already allowed herself to be foolish once, and she was not about to do such a thing again. This would have to be treated with great care, with consideration, and sensible thought rather than by giving in to her feelings which, at present, were all desperate for her to do as Lord Dorchester asked.

"That may be so, Lord Dorchester, but you cannot tell me that what was said of Lord Wileham and this bet which, for whatever reason, resulted in him being forced into my company, was untrue."

The gentleman paused then shook his head.

"No, I cannot. That was true, certainly, but there is a

good deal more to say in that regard. Please," he continued, taking a step closer to her, his voice quiet, "consider my request, at least. I shall be present for the remainder of this evening, and ready to speak with you at any time."

He turned away almost immediately, and Julianna watched him walk across the room, relieved that he had not pushed her into doing as he had requested. How different he was from the red-faced, furious fellow she had seen only a few days ago! This time, he was calm, composed, and clearly desirous to explain something to her... but she was not yet certain that she wanted to hear it.

"I do wonder what it was he was going to say to you."

Julianna looked at Lady Gilford.

"It would not be wise to allow myself to be pulled back into that situation."

"Not unless what he had to say was of great importance. There might be more to this situation than you know," Lady Thurston said, before Lady Gilford could answer, her eyes following Lord Dorchester as he moved through the crowd. "How very intriguing!"

With a sigh, Julianna turned away directly.

"I do not think that I want to hear his explanations. It is better for me to set it all to one side, to forget about Lord Wileham entirely, and to find my happiness in other things."

"But can you truly do so?" Lady Gilford slipped her arm through Julianna's again as they walked in the opposite direction from Lord Dorchester. "You have already confessed that your feelings are very strong when it comes to Lord Wileham. Can you truly put him to one side so quickly? Will you not always be thinking of what it was that Lord Dorchester wanted to say, wishing that you had heard it?"

A sudden dizziness overtook Julianna and she pulled away from both Lady Gilford and Lady Thurston.

"I – forgive me, I need some air."

Lady Gilford reached to her, with a concerned expression.

"Can we help?"

"No, no." A little choked, she backed away from them. "I need to be alone for a short while."

Turning around, she stumbled through the crowd, not quite certain where she was going. It was all becoming too much, too heavy a weight on her shoulders, too great a strain on her heart. One moment, Lady Gilford was encouraging her to forget about Lord Wileham, and the next, she was encouraging Julianna to find out more about what Lord Dorchester had to say! Her mind and body ached from being pulled in one direction and then another, making her vision blurry and her head pound as she made her way through the ballroom and then, to her relief, outside.

"My Lady, might I call your carriage?" One of the footmen by the door came out to her with a lantern in one hand and a look of concern on his face for, given the chill and the wind, it was much too cold for her to be standing out of doors. "Do you wish to take your leave?"

"Yes, yes," Julianna said, a little breathlessly. "Please, my carriage." Giving her name, she watched as the footman ran out into the gloom in search of her carriage, giving her a few moments respite. Dragging in air, she squeezed her eyes closed and let the cold bring her a little clarity. Yes, she had only just arrived, but being present at this ball, with all the gaiety and joy within it, was not the place for her, not when she was filled with such torturous thoughts. Part of her longed to go to Lord Dorchester, to have him tell her whatever it was he wanted, but the other told her to set herself apart from that completely. It would do her no good to hear stories, to learn more about Lord Wileham as what she knew already, what Lord Dorchester had confirmed to be true, was painful enough. Lord Wileham *had* been in her company simply because of a bet, and that was enough for her to know. Her desire to understand did not have to be satisfied.

"Your carriage, my Lady."

The footman reemerged, the lantern still in one hand, and offered his arm to Julianna. Grasping it quickly, Julianna allowed him to lead her back to the carriage. The coachman was already standing by the door and, as the footman helped her inside, Julianna paused before she sat down, noting something on the seat opposite.

"What is this?"

The coachman and the footman looked at her, then to what she pointed to.

"I – I do not know, my Lady." The coachman's gaze dropped away, and he shuffled his feet. "I might have taken a short rest while waiting for you, my Lady."

"Which is just as you ought," Julianna replied quickly, not wanting him to think that she was angry. "But there is a wreath opposite me and I…"

Her eyes flared as the footman's lantern illuminated the wreath a little more, and the note beside it. Begging the footman to put the lantern inside, she took the note, broke the seal, and unfolded it.

'A reminder of happier times. You have taught me a good deal more than simply how to make a wreath, Julianna. Forgive me.'

She had no need to ask who it was from. The wreath and the note were both from Lord Wileham, which meant that he was either present at the ball, or he had stopped by here in the hope that she was in attendance. Either way, he had placed this wreath and note here, and now her heart was breaking all over again.

What if there is more to this situation than you know?

Lady Thurston's words whispered back around her mind, and Julianna snatched in a breath, hot tears burning in her eyes. Dashing them away quickly before her coachman or the footman could see, she took a breath, lifted her chin, and turned again to the footman.

"Forgive me, but I think I will return to the ball."

The footman blinked but nodded, stepping back to take her hand again and help her descend the steps. Neither he nor the coachman said a single word - they did not question her about why she was already leaving the carriage she had only just called for, but Julianna did not miss the looks shared between the two men. She did not care. Suddenly, the path ahead became very clear and, the note still in her hand, she hurried back towards the townhouse.

Stepping inside, she paused only to let the music wash over her again and to search for Lord Dorchester.

He was impossible to find. The ballroom was crowded, the guests overflowing out into the gardens and the hallways – but where could he be? Gritting her teeth, Julianna stepped forward and began to move through the crowd of guests, her determination filling her.

Finally, her eyes alighted on him and, hurrying forward and heedless to those around her, she grasped his arm. Lord Dorchester turned at once, his eyes filling with surprise as he looked at her.

"I want to know," she said, her words broken by short, sharp breaths. "I want to know everything."

CHAPTER NINETEEN

*T*he way his heart lurched had reminded Andrew just how much he wanted to draw close to Lady Carsington. He had been watching her ever since her arrival – with only a few minutes away from the ballroom, so that he might place something in her carriage – and it was, to him, as though no one else was in the room. With bated breath, he had seen Lord Dorchester approaching, only for his spirits then to drop low as Lord Dorchester had taken his leave, with Lady Carsington turning away thereafter. It seemed that she was not yet willing to hear what Lord Dorchester had to say and thus, Andrew had fought the urge to give in to his low spirits and leave the ball.

What he had not expected was for Lady Carsington to rush from the ballroom so soon after Lord Dorchester had spoken to her. The urge to catch her hand, to beg her to tell him what was wrong, had been great. He had resisted but, of course, he had still gone after her, just to make certain all was well.

And now, here he was, watching her hurry back into the

townhouse, having stepped into her carriage, sat there for a short while, and then returned to the ballroom a few minutes thereafter.

Which means that she has found the wreath and the note I left for her.

Andrew did not know what to make of her response. To come back into the ballroom again, after she had found what he had left for her could mean either that she was determined to forget about him and enjoy the rest of the evening, or that she wanted to find out exactly what Lord Dorchester had to say. It had not been his intention to speak with her himself this evening, but only for her to listen to Lord Dorchester's explanation, should she be willing to. Lord Dorchester had promised that he would tell her that Andrew desired very much to speak with her also, but that would be all he said.

Now, however, Andrew could only watch and wait as Lady Carsington walked into the ballroom and, after a few moments of hesitation, walked through the crowd. It did not take Andrew long to see where she was going. Lord Dorchester turned towards her and, upon hearing Lady Carsington speak, nodded fervently and then gestured to the corner of the room.

Andrew's heart leaped. Lady Carsington was talking to Lord Dorchester. That meant that there was a little hope after all.

Making sure to stay well back, he moved to the shadows at the back of the ballroom and watched as Lord Dorchester began to talk with Lady Carsington.

I cannot see her face.

Nervousness flooded him as he made his way across the room, standing now opposite Lady Carsington but still with a few guests moving between them, simply so that he could see the expression on her face. This, he was sure, would tell him whether the dim flicker in his heart could burn and blossom into a full flame or if it ought to be extinguished.

Lady Carsington closed her eyes and shook her head, her throat working – and Andrew's shoulders tensed, his heart hitting the floor. Was she refusing to listen? Refusing to believe what was being said? Perhaps, after all of this, she was convinced that Lord Dorchester had been encouraged by Andrew to speak to her in this way in the hope that she might not think poorly of him.

Running a hand over his eyes, Andrew took a slow breath and let it out again, blowing out some of his frayed nerves with it. He could not know for certain until he spoke with Lord Dorchester, not until…

Shock ran through him as Lady Carsington's eyes caught his. He did not know where to look, frozen in place as his gaze remained tied to hers. She was looking at him steadily and, as Lord Dorchester continued to speak, he turned his head and, surprise lifting his eyebrows, nodded slowly.

Lady Carsington pressed her lips together and lifted her chin. Andrew's heart was beating painfully, his breath tying itself into a knot in his chest, lungs screaming for air. Was this to be the end of their connection? Or was he to be given a second chance, which he did not deserve?

After a few moments, Lady Carsington lifted her hand and beckoned to him – and Andrew stumbled forward. Legs weak and trembling, dread still filling him, he made his way directly across the room and stood by her, aware of how intensely she gazed at him, but finding that he could not bring himself to match it. Lowering his head, he opened his mouth, but no words came. What was he meant to say? How could he ask her if she believed what Lord Dorchester said or not?

"You left a wreath for me."

Pressing his lips tightly together, Andrew nodded, but said nothing.

"And now Lord Dorchester tells me that Lord Arthington attempted to injure you by stating a complete falsehood."

"That is so." The breathiness of his voice embarrassed him, and he cleared his throat gruffly. "I did not know anything about this."

"It occurred because Lord Arthington felt insulted by the way that Lord Wileham described his personal determination to change," Lord Dorchester put in. "I believe that Lord Arthington said one or two things which were deeply insulting towards you, Lady Carsington, and thus, Lord Wileham responded in a sharp manner before taking his leave."

Lady Carsington's eyes flashed.

"Is that so?"

"It is, but that does not excuse me, Lady Carsington," Andrew responded, quickly. "That is only one part of what took place that evening, is it not?"

She nodded, her eyes narrowed just a little, as though she were trying to ascertain whether or not he spoke honestly.

"The wreath and the note in my carriage, Lord Wileham. Why did you place them there?"

He spread his hands, aware of Lord Dorchester melting into the shadows so that he and Lady Carsington might speak freely, without his presence.

"I did not think that we would have the opportunity to speak this evening. I wanted to, I *have* been wanting to for many days, but the choice had to be yours. I have done my best to write to you repeatedly, to explain myself in one way or another, but every time that I have tried, the words have seemed stilted or false and thus, I gave up completely. It was only when Lord Dorchester came to my house – with Lord Arthington coerced into joining us – that I saw a way for my explanation to be given to you, albeit without my presence. I wanted to put the wreath and the note in your carriage because it was the only way that I could see to express my heart."

She licked her lips, her hands clasping tightly in front of her.

"And what is in your heart, Lord Wileham?"

"Regret. Pain. Sorrow." Eyes closing, he took in another breath. "I should have told you the truth about the bet and the consequences thereafter long before now. I did not do so, because I did not want to cause you pain, and I was afraid that it would push us apart." Opening his eyes, he looked at her, but Lady Carsington had dropped her head and was now looking somewhere to his left. "This has been such a strange experience for me, Lady Carsington, one which has revealed an entirely new world to my eyes. I can only apologize for the way that you found out, but what started as a bet, what began as something of a jest, has now blossomed into a beautiful gift which I shall always be grateful for, no matter what happens between us."

There came nothing but silence as his response. The music from the other end of the ballroom danced its way towards them, trying to spread the joy it brought with it to everyone's hearts, but Andrew felt nothing but apprehension. Lady Carsington might accept what he said, but still turn away from him. Perhaps he had caused her too much pain already.

"This bet." Lady Carsington lifted her gaze to his again, a steadiness there which he had not expected. "What was it?"

"It was that I could point out a young lady who had supposedly come to find herself intrigued by me." The shame of it burned heat into his face but he did not look away. "Lord Rushford had imbibed a little too much and made some foolish demands – but I can give no excuse as to my reasons for accepting the bet. I did not know the lady's face, but felt sure that I could find out who she was and thus be successful, but I was wrong. I pointed out the wrong young lady and thus, Lord Dorchester proclaimed that I could only give my attention to one young lady, instead of to as many as I wished."

"And he chose me?"

"Lord Arthington was to blame for that." Andrew winced. "I believe that I had shared with him a little about my frustrations as regarded you." Seeing her eyes flare, he explained quickly. "I did not like the fact that I could not seem to catch your attention, as I did easily with so many other young ladies. Lord Arthington thought it would be very funny indeed if I had to focus solely on you." Lady Carsington bit the edge of her lip, a frown drawing between her eyebrows. "But I found myself grateful that such consequences were placed on me," Andrew added, quickly. "My heart has never had the opportunity – I should say, I have never given it the opportunity – to grow close to anyone in particular. What I have shared with you, Lady Carsington, is something so profound that I do not think that I fully understand it! Instead of being the center of attention, instead of garnering as much interest as I might desire, instead I find myself seeking you out – and *only* you. My heart cries out for no other and, in being in your company, I find myself more than satisfied. When we are apart, I find my thoughts filled by none but you. Your kindness towards me has been immeasurable, and the guilt which swallowed me thereafter, intense. At last, now, I tell you all, Lady Carsington, though it is much too late, and I find myself without hope or expectation. My desire now is only for you and, even though you may reject me – for you have every right to do so – I shall always be grateful for what we have shared and for the happiness I have enjoyed. It has shone a new light upon my path, and I will cling to that light from this day on."

Lady Carsington took a long breath and, when she let it out, a hint of a smile crossed her lips. It was gone in a moment, but Andrew's hopes burned so fiercely, he was forced to snatch in a breath. Could it be that he might be offered another chance? That she might forgive him for his falsehoods, his lies and his pretense, and permit her heart, once more, to draw close to his?

"Will you dance with me, Lord Wileham?"

Andrew blinked, nodding fervently.

"But of course, Lady Carsington, if that is what you wish?"

"It is the waltz," she said, moving forward and putting her hand out so that it might rest on his arm. "And I think I should like to be in your arms again."

The sweetness of her words was like honey on his tongue, and it was all he could do not to sweep her up in his arms and pull her tight against him. Instead, with a bow, he offered his arm and, when she took it and her smile lifted to him, Andrew could not help himself. Turning, he caught her hand with his and lifting it gently, pressed it to his lips. Lady Carsington's eyes were like stars and when they stepped out together to dance once more, Andrew's heart was filled with such a joy, it was as though everything was brighter, sharper, and more wonderful than ever before.

CHAPTER TWENTY

*J*ulianna smiled to herself, the mistletoe berry settling between her finger and thumb. Last evening had been one of the most confusing and yet most delightful evenings of her time in London thus far and now, instead of being left with disappointment, pain and regret, her heart was happy.

"Are you quite prepared?" The door opened and Lady Thurston rushed in, her skirts billowing around her as she came into Julianna's parlor. "Goodness, you are not even dressed!"

Julianna blinked, then put the mistletoe berry back into the small, wooden box she had kept it in ever since she had taken it from the bough during her dance with Lord Wileham. Why she had not thrown it away, she did not know but now, after her conversation with Lord Wileham, she was glad that she had kept it.

"Julianna!" Lady Gilford hurried in after Lady Thurston. "We will be late! Come now, whatever have you been doing?"

"Doing?" All the more confused, Julianna rose to her

feet and looked at her friends. "I do not recall –"

"The Christmas Eve ball!" Lady Thurston clicked her tongue. "I understand that you have been deeply despondent over what has happened with Lord Wileham and your memory, therefore, must have become a little muddled."

"It has been a dreadful business." Lady Gilford shook her head. "You were absent last evening for a while and both Laura and I were eager to search for you, though after some consideration, we thought it best to permit you to recover your spirits in private. I do hope that it was not too difficult an evening. You had some enjoyment, I hope?"

"I did. And you have both been very good to me." With a smile pressing at her lips, she looked from one to the other and then took a breath before she began to explain. "However, there is something I ought to tell you both. Something which occurred last evening and will now affect my life from this day forward."

"Indeed?" Lady Gilford looked tat Lady Thurston and then frowned. "Might I ask if this is the reason you are not prepared for the Christmas Eve ball?"

"Partly, yes." Julianna cleared her throat and looked down at her gown. It was not at all the right sort of gown for her to wear to a ball, and her hair was still settled in a chignon. "I am sorry. Though I should tell you both, before you depart, that my situation with Lord Wileham has changed somewhat."

Lady Thurston and Lady Gilford glanced at each other, then looked back to Julianna.

"What do you mean?"

"I mean that there has been an understanding formed between us," Julianna replied, quietly, a smile spreading across her features as her heart leaped for sheer joy. "It is not as I thought."

Lady Gilford blinked.

"Then... he did not chase after you because of a bet?"

"No, that part is true," Julianna answered, laughing softly at Lady Gilford's confusion. "He *did* lose a bet and was requested, thereafter, to focus entirely on me. However, that has brought a great many changes to his heart and mind which he confessed to me last evening. This was after I spoke to Lord Dorchester and found out that what was said about Miss Hallstrom and Lord Wileham's attention to her was quite false. There is an explanation behind that, but it is much too convoluted to tell you about now. What I shall say, however, is that I know the truth in its entirety now, and it is not as I first thought it."

"I see." Lady Thurston plopped down on one of the chairs near Julianna, clearly a little overwhelmed by this news. Such had been the hubbub of the previous evening, Julianna had not had the opportunity to share what had happened with her friends and, even though she might have begged them to come to a quiet corner so that she could explain, it had been so overwhelming that she had required time just to take it all in. "Then... all is well?"

"All is well."

"And are you courting?" Lady Gilford asked, though Julianna quickly laughed and shook her head.

"I do not know what we shall be, or what we are, but our hearts are filled with an affection for each other which cannot be taken away," she said, quietly. "He was to call this afternoon, but the snow caused there to be some difficulty with his carriage, and he has been delayed."

"And you are now waiting for him."

Julianna nodded in answer to Lady Gilford's question.

"Hence why I quite forgot about the Christmas Eve ball. Might you forgive me?"

Lady Thurston smiled, her eyes sparkling with clear happiness over Julianna's newfound contentment.

"But of course. The roads are still clear enough for carriages to come through, however, so perhaps we shall still see you –both of you – this evening?"

"And if we do not, then we will be glad of your company tomorrow on Christmas Day," Lady Gilford put in, as Lady Thurston rose to her feet. "Pray, do tell Lord Wileham that he must join us also, if he so wishes."

Julianna smiled, rose, and embraced her friends, one after the other.

"Thank you, Marianne. Both of you have been so very kind to me, so eager to support me in my troubles and sorrows. I am truly grateful to you."

"We only wish to see you happy and settled," Lady Gilford said, squeezing Julianna's hands for a moment. "You have endured great pain already. You certainly do not need any more sorrow."

"I do hope that Lord Wileham will bring you joy." A glint came into Lady Thurston's eyes. "I also hope that his character is as altered as you say, my dear Julianna. I do not want you to have your heart broken again."

"I can assure you, I am determined to cling to this change within myself, Lady Thurston. I have every intention of becoming the very best of gentlemen."

The three ladies turned as one, and Julianna's heart leaped up into her throat only to come crashing back into her chest as Lord Wileham smiled and bowed. Much to Julianna's surprise, his dark hair appeared a little damp and when he rose from his bow, she was sure that he shivered a little.

"Forgive me for interrupting you, I could not wait another moment." Smiling, his eyes settled on Julianna, and he came towards her, though Julianna noticed the dampness on his clothes, the moisture which had settled on his skin. "My carriage's wheel was damaged earlier today and though they have done their level best to fix it, I found myself unable to wait a moment longer."

"You walked here?" Lady Thurston's voice was filled with surprise. "Goodness, you must be chilled to the bone!"

"I am." Lord Wileham laughed and grasped Julianna's outstretched hand, though she immediately shivered at how cold his fingers were. "But I could not wait another moment to see you, Lady Carsington."

"Come and stand by the fire." Urging him quickly across the room, Julianna turned her head and smiled as her friends quickly took their leave, though Lady Gilford ushered in both a maid and a footman *and* left the door to the parlor wide open, making it quite plain to Julianna that she was a little concerned about propriety.

Julianna did not care. The truth was, she was a widow and to have a gentleman with her in her townhouse was not something that was particularly scandalous, nor was it something that the *ton* would know of, given that almost everyone was either to be at this Christmas Eve ball or would stay indoors due to the inclement weather. Yes, the servants would be aware of it, and might whisper about it amongst themselves, but who else would they speak to about it? Christmas Eve and Christmas Day meant a good deal of joviality and mirth, including amongst the servants, and Julianna was certain Lord Wileham's presence would soon be forgotten.

"Fetch a brandy," she said, as the footman came closer to them both to see if he might be of aid. "And might you bring a tea tray with some hot coffee for Lord Wileham?"

The maid nodded and hurried away while the footman

crossed the room to pour a measure for Lord Wileham. The gentleman was shivering violently now and once the footman had handed Lord Wileham the brandy, Julianna asked him to stoke the fire and then sent him to fetch a blanket or two.

"You do not need to concern yourself, Julianna." Lord Wileham smiled gently though his face was white against his dark hair. "I am quite all right, just a little damp and cold."

"You are trembling with the cold," she stated, coming to sit by Lord Wileham as the fire blazed next to him. "Why ever did you walk here when the weather is so severe? There was no need. I would have waited for you."

"My heart would not let me wait."

The soft smile which curved his lips sent a sweetness straight into her heart and she sighed contently, wishing that she could lean against him, but aware that the footman and the maid were soon to arrive.

"Then I am glad to see you," she answered, reaching across so that she might take his hand in hers, though her stomach dropped at just how cold it was still. "Though I fear we will be unable to attend the Christmas Eve ball, given how you are at present."

"I had no thought of the Christmas Eve ball," he told her, with a quiet laugh as the footman returned with the blankets. "Is that why Lady Thurston and Lady Gilford were present?"

Julianna nodded, standing up so that the footman could place the blankets around Lord Wileham.

"They expected me to be quite prepared and ready to join them, though when they walked in I could not recall why they had come to call. Lady Thurston berated me about my lack of appropriate attire, and it was only then that I remembered about the Christmas Eve ball. I had not told them about our change in circumstances and thus, I believe that they both were concerned for my present state of mind and were eager to take me to the Christmas Eve ball."

"They are very good friends, I think."

"They are," Julianna agreed, with a smile as the footman stepped back, ready to take any more orders from Julianna, though she quickly dismissed him. "They have been present by my side ever since I returned to London, and were eager to support me in my distress."

"Which came by my hand."

"But which we do not need to discuss any longer," Julianna said softly, not wishing to bring up the difficulties they had shared previously. "Come now, drink your brandy so that I may stop fretting about you."

Lord Wileham chuckled, but did as he was bade and, within a few minutes, some color began to draw itself back across his features. His hair no longer clung damply to his forehead, he stopped shivering, and the paleness in his face began to dissipate.

"You see?" he said, and she smiled at him as the maid set the tray on the table next to Julianna, "I am recovered."

"You are beginning to recover," Julianna stated, firmly. "There will be coffee once you are ready."

Lord Wileham smiled softly.

"Thank you, Julianna. Again, you prove your kind, sweet nature to me by showing me such great consideration, even though it is I who have inconvenienced you by walking to your house and thereafter, shivering and trembling with the cold!"

"It is no inconvenience." Her eyes took him in, and she let her gaze linger, seeing the way that the sides of his eyes crinkled as he smiled at her. There was a softness about his features which she had not seen before, a tenderness in his expression which spoke to her heart. "I have cared for you once before, Lord Wileham, and I am more than able to do so again."

His smile grew, his eyes twinkling.

"I am grateful for that. We have traversed a great many difficulties, have we not? All at my own hand, I admit, and I would apologize for them again had I any belief that you would accept such words from me!"

Laughing, she shook her head.

"I have told you that there is no need for such apologies to be given again, Wileham. What you have already said is what I have accepted and thus, there is no reason for you to consider the past any longer. I am grateful for your explanations, gratified by them in fact, but there is no desire in me to linger on what has happened. Rather, I would like to consider the future."

"As would I." Lord Wileham took a deep breath, then let it out, his shoulders settling. "I suppose we have not talked about the future yet. I have been so busy considering the past and how to make amends that I have not permitted myself to consider what might be possible for me in the future."

Julianna handed him a cup of coffee, though the intensity of his gaze as he looked back at her had her stomach twisting this way and that, anticipation flowing through her veins and quickening her heart. She dared not sit next to him, not now, not yet. Their paths had been separate, but now they had to walk together, into whatever it was that the future held for them.

"Now, mayhap, we might talk of the future together?"

"I should like that," Julianna answered, aware of how

quickly her words tumbled out of her. "If we are set on this venture together, Lord Wileham, then let us consider what our next step is."

"Courtship?" Lord Wileham suggested, then laughed somewhat ruefully. "You must forgive me, Julianna. To be in this state of affairs is something that I never even *considered* before. I have always been so eager to push aside every young lady, to have them eager for my affections while hiding my heart from them entirely, that I have never once even thought about what I should do, should my heart decide to cling to another."

"And now?" she asked, softly, sitting down opposite him rather than beside him. "Do you desire courtship?"

Lord Wileham considered, and Julianna's heart plummeted to the ground, wondering why he might be thinking over such matters with such deliberation. Was it that he did not want to court her? Was something wrong?

"No, Julianna, I do not want courtship."

She closed her eyes, tears beginning to burn behind her eyes.

"I see."

The quaver in her voice was unmistakable and, as she opened her eyes to look at him again, she saw how his eyes flared.

"Oh, no, no!" Setting aside his coffee, he threw off his blankets and hurried towards her, reaching out to grasp her hands in his, falling to his knees before her so that he might look up into her face. "My dear Julianna, that is not what I meant! Of *course,* I should be glad to court you, though that is not what I desire."

Julianna let out a slightly broken laugh, sniffing as she fought to keep her tears back.

"I do not know what you are trying to say, Wileham."

He smiled, reaching up to caress her cheek.

"Forgive my foolish explanations. The reason I say that I do not want courtship is because I desire something more profound, something greater – something *stronger* – than that."

The tears quickly returned but this time, it was not from distress, but from a fierce and sudden understanding of what it was that he desired.

"Oh." Blinking rapidly, she tried to smile. "You want something more?"

"I think – I think I should like to marry you." Lord Wileham's eyes flared as if he himself was surprised by his own desires. "Good gracious, can that be so?" His head dropping forward, he let his hand lower from her cheek and instead, found her other free hand and took it in his, a breath escaping from him. "Good gracious. This is most astonishing."

She laughed then, freeing her hands from his and instead, pressing them lightly against his face so that he had no choice but to look up at her.

"You sound astonished, Wileham. I believe it is the young lady who ought to be overcome with amazement in this moment rather than the gentleman who is meant to be doing the asking!"

He grinned at her, the movement causing a slight scratch of his cheek against her soft hands.

"I believe that you are quite right. However, these circumstances are so unexpected, I confess myself to be a little bewildered at just how much I find myself desiring to be wed to you." The grin faded a little, the tenderness in his eyes softening his expression. "My dear Julianna, when I was first given this consequence, I was both frustrated and irritated with my friends and with myself. Now, however, I am grateful for what it has given me – for what *you* have given me. I have discovered a happiness which nothing else has ever been able to match, a joy which is so much a part of me that I do not think it will ever leave. When I thought us separated, there was so great a pain in my heart, I was certain that it would be broken for the rest of my days. To know that now, we stand here together and look to our future as husband and wife is astonishing to me. It is wonderful, beautiful, and utterly extraordinary. I do not think that I could endure a day apart from you, Julianna, and in this moment, as I look into your eyes, I see my future reflected there and it is a beautiful one indeed, for I will be there with you."

Julianna's throat constricted as emotions poured over her, binding her heart so tightly to his, she knew that it could never be pulled apart. Lord Wileham smiled up into her eyes, his fingers threading through hers, and Julianna wanted to fling herself into his arms, to give herself up to everything she felt and embrace everything that he offered.

"There is one thing that you have not yet done, Wileham," she said, softly, as a slight frown puckered his forehead. "I do not think that you have asked me to marry you yet."

The broad smile made her laugh and when he rose to his feet, she went with him, her hands still captured in his.

"Then let me remedy that at this very moment," he said, looking down at her, though his smile disappeared to make way for the solemnity of what he was asking her. "My dear Julianna, you are the only one who has captured my heart. I desire nothing more than to be your husband and for you to be my bride. Since I met you, I have been confused, lost, my heart torn into pieces and then put back together again, whole and better than it was before. I cannot think of being apart from you and, even now, the thought of courtship seems too insignificant, given the feelings which I possess – the burning of my heart, the clamoring of my soul when it comes to you, Julianna, means that I can do nothing more than this: ask you if you will consider being my bride." With a smile, he lifted her hand and then kissed the back of it, his eyes never leaving hers. "I shall never go back to the gentleman I was before, not now that my heart is tied to yours. Will you marry me, Julianna? Will you be my wife? If you consent, I shall be the happiest gentleman in all of England – perhaps even in all the world – and this Christmas shall be the brightest I have ever experienced."

"How could I say no?" Julianna asked quietly, tears building again, but this time, she did not force them back, did not steady herself but let the tears flow. "To hear such words from your lips brings my heart such happiness, such contentment and joy, that I cannot refuse what it demands of me. Yes, of course, I shall marry you, Wileham. I *shall* be your wife."

Lord Wileham closed his eyes, his smile spreading slowly across his face, his shoulders dropping in evident relief as though he had, for whatever reason, been expecting her to refuse, or to ask him to wait a little longer. Julianna smiled softly, looking up at him and, boldly, took her hand from his to settle it against his heart.

"We shall belong together, you and I," she murmured, as he finally opened his eyes again. "From this moment on until the end of our days, we shall be as one."

"That is all that I desire," he whispered, and began to lower his lips towards hers.

Shocking him, so that he let out a groan, Julianna quickly pulled away, slipping her hands from his, for she had remembered something. Lord Wileham let out another low groan from the back of his throat, the sound practically demanding that she turn back to him. With hastening steps, she crossed the room, picked up the small, wooden box and then returned to him with it, a broad smile on her face.

"I saved this," she told him, opening the lid to reveal the one white mistletoe berry. "Do you recall?"

Lord Wileham nodded slowly, his eyes a little rounded with surprise.

"It came from the time we danced together."

"It is to be exchanged for a kiss, is it not?" Smiling, she leaned against him again, still holding the mistletoe berry in one hand, lifting it up to him. "And I told you it was to be done at a time of my choosing."

His eyes flickered.

"I recall."

"Then consider this a time of my choosing, Lord Wileham."

Lord Wileham did not grasp her at once, as she had expected. He did not fling his arms around her, crush her against him and press his lips to hers as she had expected. Instead, he took a breath, nodded, smiled, and then took the mistletoe berry from her hand. Looking at it for a moment, he set it down and then moved a little closer. One arm wrapped around her waist, and his head dropped but his lips still did not find hers. With his eyes meeting hers, and his other hand resting against her cheek, brushing lightly against her skin, he smiled tenderly, as though this was the first opportunity that he had ever had to hold her so close.

"I love you, Julianna."

His words shot like lightning through her, and she caught her breath, her eyes wide.

"This may come as an even greater astonishment to you," he continued, with a chuckle, evidently seeing the surprise in her face, "but I believe that this is what I feel for you. I am completely and utterly lost in love, wishing to tie myself only to you for the remainder of my days, and now that we are to be husband and wife, I do not think that there will ever be any greater happiness for me."

"Oh, Wileham." Her heart soared and she wrapped her arms around his neck, pulling herself even closer to him. "I love you in return."

With those words still on her lips, Lord Wileham dropped his head and captured her mouth, just as he had captured her heart. He kissed her carefully at first, as though he were unsure of himself, only to then tilt his head to deepen their kiss. Julianna lost herself in it, gave herself up to him entirely, and then clung to him as though she could never bear to let him go.

"My wonderful Julianna," he whispered, his lips barely leaving hers. "You have made this Christmas the most joyous one there has ever been. I love you desperately. I love you with all of myself and I swear to you, I shall never let you go."

I AM so glad everything worked out between Julianna and Lord Wileham. She was generous to forgive him so quickly but it is working for her!

Please check out the first book of the Christmas Kisses series, A Lady's Christmas Kiss. The Lady's Christmas Kiss

READ ahead a few pages for a Sneak Peek!

MY DEAR READER

Thank you for reading and supporting my books! I hope this story brought you some escape from the real world into the always captivating Regency world. A good story, especially one with a happy ending, just brightens your day and makes you feel good! If you enjoyed the book, would you leave a review on Amazon? Reviews are always appreciated.

Below is a complete list of all my books! Why not click and see if one of them can keep you entertained for a few hours?

The Duke's Daughters Series
The Duke's Daughters: A Sweet Regency Romance Boxset
A Rogue for a Lady
My Restless Earl
Rescued by an Earl
In the Arms of an Earl
The Reluctant Marquess (Prequel)

A Smithfield Market Regency Romance
The Smithfield Market Romances: A Sweet Regency Romance Boxset
The Rogue's Flower
Saved by the Scoundrel
Mending the Duke
The Baron's Malady

The Returned Lords of Grosvenor Square
The Returned Lords of Grosvenor Square: A Regency Romance Boxset
The Waiting Bride
The Long Return
The Duke's Saving Grace
A New Home for the Duke

The Spinsters Guild
The Spinsters Guild: A Sweet Regency Romance Boxset
A New Beginning
The Disgraced Bride
A Gentleman's Revenge
A Foolish Wager
A Lord Undone

Convenient Arrangements
Convenient Arrangements: A Regency Romance Collection
A Broken Betrothal
In Search of Love
Wed in Disgrace
Betrayal and Lies
A Past to Forget
Engaged to a Friend

Landon House
Landon House: A Regency Romance Boxset
Mistaken for a Rake
A Selfish Heart
A Love Unbroken
A Christmas Match
A Most Suitable Bride

An Expectation of Love

Second Chance Regency Romance
Second Chance Regency Romance Boxset
Loving the Scarred Soldier
Second Chance for Love
A Family of her Own
A Spinster No More

Soldiers and Sweethearts
To Trust a Viscount
Whispers of the Heart
Dare to Love a Marquess
Healing the Earl
A Lady's Brave Heart

Ladies on their Own: Governesses and Companions
Ladies on their Own Boxset
More Than a Companion
The Hidden Governess
The Companion and the Earl
More than a Governess
Protected by the Companion

Lost Fortunes, Found Love
A Viscount's Stolen Fortune
For Richer, For Poorer
Her Heart's Choice
A Dreadful Secret
Their Forgotten Love
His Convenient Match

Only for Love

The Heart of a Gentleman
A Lord or a Liar
The Earl's Unspoken Love
The Viscount's Unlikely Ally
The Highwayman's Hidden Heart
Miss Millington's Unexpected Suitor

Christmas Stories
Love and Christmas Wishes: Three Regency Romance Novellas
A Family for Christmas
Mistletoe Magic: A Regency Romance
Heart, Homes & Holidays: A Sweet Romance Anthology

Christmas Kisses Series
Christmas Kisses Box Set
The Lady's Christmas Kiss
The Viscount's Christmas Queen
Her Christmas Duke

Happy Reading!
All my love,
Rose

A SNEAK PEEK OF A LADY'S CHRISTMAS KISS

PROLOGUE

"*I* have wonderful news!"

Rebecca looked up at her mother, but then immediately turned her head away. Lady Wilbram often came with news and, much of the time, it was nothing more than idle gossip; something that Rebecca herself did not enjoy listening to.

"Yes, Mama?" She did not so much as even look up from her embroidery, but rather continued to sew. The long, bleak winter stretched out before her, dreary and dismal – much like the state of her heart at present – and with very little to cheer her. Her father, the Earl of Wilbram, had made it clear that he was not to go to London for the little Season and thus, Rebecca was to be stuck at home, having only her mother for company. No doubt there would be a great deal more of this sort of occurrence, whereby her mother would burst into the room, expressing great delight at some news or other and, in doing so, remind Rebecca of just how far away she was from it all.

Although I am not certain that I wish to return to

London at present. There is the chance that he would be there and I do not think I could bear to see him.

"Rebecca. You are not as much as even listening to me!"

Out of the corner of her eye, Rebecca caught how her mother threw up her hands, but merely smiled quietly. "I am paying you a *great* deal of attention, Mother," she answered, silently thinking to herself that it was the only thing she *could* do, given just how determined her mother was. Having been quite contented with her own thoughts, it was a little frustrating to have been interrupted so.

"You shall soon drop your embroidery once you realize what it is I have to tell you." The promise in her mother's voice was one that finally caught Rebecca's interest, but telling herself not to be foolish, she threw only a quick smile in her mother's direction.

"Yes, I am sure I shall," she promised softly. "Please, tell me what it is. I am almost beside myself with anticipation." Her sarcasm obviously laid heavy on her mother's shoulders, for she immediately threw up her hands in clear disgust.

"Well, if you must behave so, then I shall not tell you the contents of this letter. You shall not know of it! And *I* shall be the one to go to the Duke's Christmas... affair."

Rebecca blinked, her gaze still fixed down upon her embroidery, but her hand stilling on the needle. Had she heard her mother correctly? Had she, in fact, said the words Duke and Christmas? Her stomach tightened perceptively, and she looked up, her irritation suddenly forgotten.

"*Now* I have your attention."

Her mother's eyebrows lifted and Rebecca set her embroidery down completely, her hands going to her lap. "Yes, Mama, now you have my attention," This was said rather quickly and with a slight flippancy, which Rebecca was certain her mother would hear in her voice, but she did not seem to respond. Seeing her mother's shoulders drop after a moment, her hands going to her sides again, Rebecca let out a slow breath. Evidently, she was forgiven already.

"Yes, I did say the Duke – the Duke of Meyrick, in fact – and I *did* say Christmas."

"What is it he has invited us to?"

"A Christmas house party. It is a little unusual, for it appears to be longer than many others would be. But then again, I suppose as the Duke of Meyrick, he is quite able to do as he pleases!"

"How wonderful!" In an instant, the grey winter seemed to fade from her eyes, no longer held out before her as the only path she had to take. Instead, she had an opportunity for happiness, enjoyment, laughter and smiles – as well as the fact that there would be very little chance of being in company with *him*. No doubt he was either back at his estate or would return to London for the little Season.

"We shall have to speak to your father, of course."

At this, Rebecca's heart plunged to the ground, splintering as it fell. Her father had only just declared that he would remain at his estate over the winter. Even if there *was* an invitation to a most prestigious house party, the chances of him agreeing to attend were very small indeed. Scowling up at her mother, she turned her head away. Why had she told her something such as this only for it to be snatched away again?

"Even if your father should not wish to attend, there is no reason you and I cannot both go," her mother continued immediately, turning Rebecca's scowl into a smile of delight. "He will understand – and given that his estate is not very far from our own, the journey will not be a difficult one. Besides which, it is an excellent occasion for you to make further acquaintances in preparation for the summer season... that is, unless you have any desire to find a gentleman suitor this Christmas."

Rebecca laughed, shaking her head at her mother's twinkling eyes and forcing herself not to think of *him*. Given that her mother and father knew nothing about the affair and, therefore, the abrupt ending to what had taken place, she did not think it wise to inform them of it. "Mama, I am very glad indeed we have been invited. I go with no expectation, just as you ought to do."

Lady Wilbram smiled warmly. "You are quite correct. Now we must make preparations to attend this house party. You will need to look through your gowns and decide which of them is the most suitable. We have time to purchase one or two new gowns also, for there is certain to be at least one Christmas ball! You must be prepared for every possible occasion." Making her way back towards the door with purposeful steps, as though she intended to begin such preparations immediately, Lady Wilbram threw a glance back at Rebecca. Understanding that she was meant to go after her mother, Rebecca set her embroidery down and followed immediately, her heart light and filled with hope.

"Prepared for every occasion, Mama?" she asked as her mother nodded firmly. "What exactly is it that I ought to expect from such a house party? I have only been to one before and it lasted only three days. There was very little that could be done by way of occasion."

"You will find the Duke's house parties are very different experiences," her mother told her, grasping her hand warmly as they walked through the door. "You must have every expectation and, at the same time, no expectation. That is why we must be prepared for every eventuality, making certain that you have an outfit suitable for whatever it is the Duke might decide to do. Christmas is such a wonderful season, is it not?"

Rebecca laughed softly at her mother's excited expression and the delight in her voice. "Made all the more wonderful by this house party," she agreed, wondering how she was going to contain her anticipation for the few weeks before the house party began. "I am looking forward to it. It seems as though winter will not be so mediocre after all."

CHAPTER ONE

After being introduced to everyone, Rebecca took her seat beside her very dear friend, Miss Augusta Moir, whom she was very glad to see. They had exchanged letters quite frequently, and when news of the house party reached Rebecca, one of the first things she did had been to write to Augusta. How glad she was to receive Augusta's letter back, and how delighted to know that she would also be present!

"And that is almost all of us!" Lady Meyrick put her hands out wide, welcoming them all. "There are only one or two other guests still to arrive. I do not know why they have been delayed, but that does not mean we cannot continue. We will soon begin our festivities and they will join us when they are able. Pray, enjoy your conversations for a few minutes longer and, thereafter, the first of our games will begin!"

Rebecca glanced around the room, looking at each and every face and recognizing only a few of them. She did not know exactly who else would arrive, but the company here seemed to be quite delightful. In addition to the fact that she had her dear friend Augusta present also, she was quite convinced it would be an excellent few weeks.

"I do wonder what such festivities will be," Speaking in a hushed whisper, Miss Moir leaned towards Rebecca. "I have heard the Duke is something of an extravagant fellow. Perhaps that will mean this holiday house party will be an exceptional one."

"Yes, but *all* Dukes are known to be extravagant fellows," Rebecca reminded her friend, chuckling. "I would expect nothing less. Although," she continued. "I do wonder where the Duke himself is."

"Did you not greet him when you arrived? He was waiting on the steps to make certain that we were greeted. I certainly was made to feel very welcome by his mother!"

"Yes, he did do so." Remembering the slightly pinched expression on the Duke's face when he had greeted both her and her mother, Rebecca allowed her own concern to remain. "He did not appear to be very glad to see us, however. I will say that for him."

Her friend nodded slowly, her gaze drifting around the room as murmurs of conversation continued between the other guests. "He did not smile once, and certainly I found him rather stiff. His mother, on the other hand, was quite the opposite."

"Mayhap he simply does not like the cold, and given the Season, it is rather cold."

Her friend nodded in agreement, although Rebecca did not miss the twinkle in her friend's eyes. "It is almost as though he does not realize it is wintertime," she remarked, making Rebecca laugh. Her laughter changed into a sigh. "Perhaps he is as I am, in waiting and hoping for the summer to return," Her mind grew suddenly heavy, and she looked away. "I confess I struggle with this long winter. My mood is much improved now that my father has permitted me to come to this house party, however."

Miss Moir laughed softly. "And I am also grateful for your presence here. I am, as you know, a little shy, and I confess that not knowing a great many people here as yet has allowed my anxiety to rise a little."

"You have no need to be at all anxious," Rebecca replied firmly. "You are more than handsome, come from an excellent family and you are well able to have many a conversation with both gentlemen and ladies." She lifted one eyebrow. "At times, I think you pretend this anxiety is a part of your character, for I do not think I would be aware of it otherwise."

"I swear to you, I do not pretend!" Miss Moir exclaimed, only to let out a chuckle and to shake her head, realizing that Rebecca was teasing her. "Do you hope to meet anyone of interest here? Or shall you only be interested in furthering your acquaintances? Christmas is a time where many a gentleman will seek to steal a kiss!"

Hesitating, Rebecca wondered how she was to answer. Her friend was entirely unaware of how her heart had been broken this last Season. Indeed, neither her mother nor her father was aware of it either, but she had borne this heavy weight for many months. The pain lingered still, and there was only one gentleman that she was to blame for it. Her mother and her friends might be hopeful that she would acquaint herself with a gentleman of note with the hope that perhaps the match would be made in the summer Season, but for the present, Rebecca was quite contented to have only acquaintances – and nothing more. Her heart was still too damaged. It certainly had not been healed enough for her to even *think* about becoming closely acquainted with another gentleman.

"Lady Rebecca?"

Rebecca blinked quickly, and then silently demanded that she smile in response. "Forgive me, I became a little lost in thought." Shrugging, she looked away. "I think I should be glad of new acquaintances for the present at least. I do not want nor require anything else."

"I quite understand," Miss Moir looked away, just as Rebecca turned her gaze back towards her friend. Rebecca chose to say nothing further, waiting until her friend looked back at her before she continued the conversation.

"What do you think shall be our first game?" With a quick breath, she returned their topic of conversation to the house party itself. She did not want to go into any particular details about what had happened the previous season, given that a good deal of it was still a secret.

Miss Moir clapped her hands lightly. "I do hope it will be something that will make us all laugh and smile so that there is no awkwardness between any of us any longer." Excitement shone in her eyes, and Rebecca could not help but smile.

"Perhaps there will be some Christmas games! Out of all the ones you can think of, which one would be your favorite?"

The two considered this for some minutes and, thereafter, fell into a deep discussion about whether the Twelfth Night cake or Snapdragon was the very best game. But eventually, their conversation was cut short by Lady Meyrick speaking again.

"I do not think we shall wait any longer. Instead, we shall proceed to the library – but not to dance or any such thing! No indeed, there shall be *many* a game at this house party! Yes, we are to be provided with a great deal of entertainment during your time here, but on occasion we shall be required to make our own entertainment... as we shall do this evening."

Chuckling good naturedly, Rebecca grinned as Miss Moir looped her arm through hers so they might walk together. It appeared this was to be the beginning of a most excellent holiday.

"Do you know who it is that is yet to arrive?" Rebecca asked quietly, as Lady Meyrick spoke quietly to her son, who had interrupted her for some reason.

"No, I do not know," Miss Moir shot her a glance. "But I, myself, would not *dare* to be tardy to something such as this, not when the Duke and his mother have shown such generosity!"

Rebecca shrugged. "Mayhap those still absent are well known to the Duke and had always stated they would be tardy?"

"Mayhap," Miss Moir looked around the room at each guest in turn as they waited to make their way to the library. "I admit I am eager to know who else is to arrive!"

"As am I." Rebecca grinned at her friend just as Lady Meyrick clapped her hands brightly, catching everyone's attention again. The bright smile on the lady's face reflected the joy and anticipation in Rebecca's heart as she waited to hear what it was they were to do.

"We shall begin by playing ourselves a few hands of cards. However, it shall be a little different, for there will be forfeits for those who lose, but gifts for the winner!"

This was met by murmurs of excitement as Rebecca's heart skipped a beat in a thrill of anticipation. She was already looking forward to the game, wondering whether she would have any chance of winning, and if she did, what the gift she would receive might be. A million ideas went through her mind as she battled to catch her breath. There was often a good deal less consideration to propriety and society's customs at such occasions, according to her mother. They were a good deal freer, no longer bound by a set of strict and rigid rules. This was a chance to laugh, to make merry and to enjoy every moment of being here. She was already looking forward to it.

"If you would like to make your way through to the library, the card tables have already been set out."

Unwilling to show any great eagerness for fear of being teased about it by either her mother or her friend, Rebecca stood quietly but did not move.

"Come!" Miss Moir immediately moved forward, tugging Rebecca along with her. "What do you suppose the forfeits might be?"

Rebecca laughed as they made to quit of the room. "I confess I can think of a great many things, but I cannot be certain whether I am correct!"

Miss Moir bit her lip. "I do hope I shall not fail. I would be most embarrassed should I make a fool of myself."

Rebecca pressed her friend's hand. "I do not think you need to have any fear in that regard, my dear friend. The forfeits will not be severe. They may make us a little embarrassed, but it is all in good humor. At least, that is what my mother has told me!"

At this, Miss Moir let out a long breath. "I understand. There will be nothing of any severity."

"Nothing." Rebecca smiled as she walked into the library. "Absolutely. In fact, I do believe there will be nothing in all the time we reside here that should bring you any shame, embarrassment, upset, or anger."

With a smile still upon her face, she walked directly into the room, only to come to a sudden halt. To her utter horror, she perceived a gentleman standing directly opposite her, a gentleman whom she recognized immediately but whom she had vowed never to see again. Her breath hitched as she looked directly at him.

Surely it could not be. Fate would not be so cruel to demand this of her, would not take such a happy occasion and quite ruin it by his presence, would it? And yet, it appeared she was to have such misfortune, for the one gentleman sitting there was the one who had broken her heart. The gentleman who had taken all from her, who had left her with nothing – and at the end, begged her to keep it from the ears and eyes of the *ton*. A gentleman who now went pale as he realized who she was, a shadow in his eyes as he looked at her.

And everything suddenly went very cold indeed.

Oh, no! It seems someone from her past was invited to the house party...someone she didn't want to see again! Check out the rest of the story in the Kindle store The Lady's Christmas Kiss

JOIN MY MAILING LIST

Sign up for my newsletter to stay up to date on new releases, contests, giveaways, freebies, and deals!

Free book with signup!

Monthly Facebook Giveaways! Books and Amazon gift cards!
Join me on Facebook: https://www.facebook.com/rosepearsonauthor

Website: www.RosePearsonAuthor.com

Follow me on Goodreads: Author Page

Printed in Dunstable, United Kingdom